W9-ALN-989

THE MEASURE OF JUSTICE

Also by the Author

Wager
Hunter's Stand

THE MEASURE OF JUSTICE

Steven Linder

Walker and Company
New York

For Jenny and Stacy, who make me proud.

First published in the United States of America in 1992
by Walker Publishing Company, Inc.

Published simultaneously in Canada by Thomas Allen & Son
Canada, Limited, Markham, Ontario

Library of Congress Cataloging-in-Publication Data
Linder, Steven.
The measure of justice / Steven Linder.
p.   cm.
ISBN 0-8027-4134-7 (cloth)
I. Title.
PS3562.I51118M4   1992
813'.54—dc20   92-11520
CIP

Printed in the United States of America

2   4   6   8   10   9   7   5   3   1

THE MEASURE OF JUSTICE

CHAPTER 1

GATHERING thunderheads veiled the sunset and a black cloud shadow plunged down the mountain slopes, spilling across the town in the foothills below. The wind turned raw and its bite sent dogs scratching under the boardwalks. People stopped in the middle of their business and stared up at the sky, all of them in the same breathless pose.

Dan Callum felt the chill pass over and stopped with his hammer in midswing. He looked up in time to see darkness fall over the hills east of town.

"What you think, Pa?" The boy was worried but trying not to show it. Callum smiled to put his son at ease.

"A storm coming, for sure," he said. "Time enough to finish here, though."

"Think it'll come a twister?"

Callum stared at the clouds thoughtfully. "No, not this time. I can feel rain in it."

"That a good sign, is it?"

"Usually is. Hand me the rest of those nails and get yourself back home. I'll be along once I tack down these boards. Liable to have a blow. Can't have them tearing loose in the wind."

"I want to stay and help you."

"No, son. Run along like I told you. Those clouds are going to open up a soaker any minute. Your ma will skin me good if I let you catch a chill. Move along, now."

Grudgingly, Randy Callum handed his father the box of nails. "You promise you won't be long?"

"Have your ma put coffee on. I'll be home before it's brewed."

1

Randy watched his father take one more look at the threatening sky and quickly get back to work, his hammer crashing like thunder. Then the boy screwed his hat down tight and took off in a dead run.

"*Straight* home," Callum yelled after him. "You hear me?"

Randy veered round the Union Hall, still running strong as he struck down Bannon's main street. The weekly mule train that carried supplies to the mining camps was tied off outside the hotel. Usually, he would have lingered to study the harnessed teams, gawk at the riches of foodstuffs and dry goods stacked high on the wagons. Listening to the drivers talk about their teams and the steep trails was nearly as much fun as dreaming about the cargo they hauled. He almost always learned a good new swear word or two when the drivers were in town.

But his father's warnings were not to be taken lightly, so he ran by, feeling virtuous for resisting temptation.

The local businesses were already closing up; men were drifting home to wait out the coming storm. A small crowd had gathered outside the saloon, men drinking beer and watching the clouds, swapping tales of storms from years ago. In a quiet town like Bannon, weather was a topic folks never tired of. Wagering was a close second in favored activities. And since they knew nothing else quite so well as the weather, that was often what they wagered on. A good thunderstorm could seem like a real sporting event.

Gus Barker, an ancient mule skinner with a beard down to his breast buttons, was holding his own among the yarn swappers. When Randy drew near, the old man yelled out, "Hey, boy! How'd you like to earn yourself some spending money?"

Randy skidded to a stop in front of him. "How's that?"

Barker dug around in a pouch at his belt, then held out a shiny nickel. "This-here all for yourself."

"What I got to do for it?" Randy asked.

Barker and his crowd flashed stained teeth. "We got us a

bet," the mule skinner said, sweeping a hand toward his grinning buddies. "And we need a impartial judge to name the winner. You got the look to me of a fair, honest man."

"That's so, I suppose," Randy said proudly.

"Here's what you do, boy. Couldn't be easier, just stand right where you are now."

"Here? In the middle of the street?"

"That's right," Barker said.

"And do what?"

"We got us a bet over the exact second the rain starts. Jimmy here says it's gonna come in five minutes. Earl, he thinks it's gonna hold off another half hour."

"Damned right it is," Earl Vickers, a clerk in the town bank, mumbled. He swayed side to side and focused on Randy without blinking; it was clear he had a good start on the night's drinking. "What we need, young Callum, is for you to be our scout. Think you can do that?"

Randy scratched his head over that a bit. "A rain scout?"

"Right," Barker said. "Jest stand there and tell us the very second you feel a raindrop light on you. That's all you gotta do to earn this-here nickel."

"How I know for sure you'll give it to me after I stood here and got rained on?"

"You don't think I'd cheat you, do you, boy?"

Randy studied the old man's face. "I don't know," he said. "I don't know you that well."

The other men laughed. "That's a smart kid you picked, all right, mule man. Smarter maybe than you."

Barker frowned. "Tell you what I'll do, boy." He set the coin atop a hitching post. "I'll leave it right here in plain sight. And when you feel that first raindrop strike you, you just race over and grab it. That will be the signal and we'll know then to call time."

"I don't know," Randy said, edging closer. The shiny coin was a powerful lure. "It don't seem like much for standing out here and getting soaked. Ma won't like it if I come home wet."

"See here," Barker snapped, "that's good money for a brat your age. It's no use tryin' to hoist the price on me. That's all you get."

"Maybe I don't want to be judge. Maybe I wanna be in on the bet."

The mule skinner shook his head. "It's not right to have no boy gambling. Your pa might not like it."

One of the men poked Barker in the ribs. "C'mon, let him play along."

"Sure, why not?" the others joined in.

Vickers laughed harshly. "Just more for me when I win."

"All right, all right," Barker grumbled. He turned back to Randy. "You got yer own money to put up?"

"Yessir, a nickel."

The men laughed some more at that. "This boy's got more surprises in him than one of your mules, old-timer."

"Good enough. He's in."

"Yeah, let him play."

Barker sneered at them. He grudgingly stuck out his hand. "Okay, let's see your money."

Randy dug into the pockets of his trousers. He fished around a little longer, searching deep.

"C'mon, kid. You got it or ain't you?"

"It's just well hid is all. It's here, got it right here." And he slapped his hand down on the post.

"So what time you want, boy?" Vickers asked impatiently.

That's when Randy pulled his hand back, snatching Barker's nickel from the post. "Now!" he cried.

Then he turned and bolted down the street before any of them could fathom what had happened.

There was a moment of stunned silence, followed by a stream of curses. Barker lurched out on the street after him. "Damn you, boy. Your pa will hear about this. So help me, I'll—"

Then he stopped in his tracks and batted his hand as if brushing a fly. He stared at pockmarks appearing in the dust. "Well, I'll be," he grunted. "It's raining."

And it was. Fat raindrops plunked down around him, sounding closer and closer together until, just seconds later, the sky opened up for real.

The men behind Barker sang out in a chorus of laughter. "Come in out of the wet, old man. Appears you owe us *all* a drink."

By that time, Randy was too far gone to worry about Barker catching him. He cut behind the stables and stopped there to get his breath. It wasn't likely Barker would chase after him, but he figured to stay low just in case. It was safe here, though, and he decided to take a minute and savor victory. He held up his new nickel and turned it over and over, watching it gleam like a priceless gem.

The rain was steady now, hard pelting drops that banged on the roof like pellets of gravel. Reluctantly he tucked away his prize and got back to his feet. Home was on the northwest edge of town, a good two hundred yards away. But the rain had driven everyone inside; by sneaking around back of the stables and cutting through Jim Peterson's yard, he figured to make it without being spotted.

Randy crept out from his hiding place and looked around. No one to be seen. Bannon was quiet as a ghost town. But he had barely stepped away from the stables when a bolt of lightning lit up the sky. And shone on a figure not ten feet away.

Randy stopped so short he stumbled and nearly fell. It spooked him so bad, it was all he could do to keep from shouting out loud. The apparition had materialized from nowhere!

Before him was a huge black horse, and atop it a powerful figure with the chest and shoulders of a man . . . but no face! The lightning faded, and with it, the nightmarish thing vanished into shadow.

He stood rooted by fear. The hair rose on his neck and cold, clammy sweat ran down his spine. A *ghost!* It had to be a ghost. Nothing else could have sneaked up so quiet.

Randy started to tremble. He wanted to run, but his legs had gone soft and quivery.

"Don't be afraid, boy. I won't hurt you."

It took a moment for Randy to believe what he'd heard. The voice was soft, even gentle sounding. The man urged his mount closer, then looking down at Randy, he pushed back the hood that had shrouded his face. Once, two priests from a French monastery had stayed overnight in Bannon, passing through on a journey they called a pilgrimage. They had worn cloaks like this stranger's, loose wool coats with a peaked hood and billowing sleeves.

The man—not a ghost, Randy was relieved to see—had hair and a full beard all of silver, as pale as the coin in Randy's pocket.

The stranger leaned an elbow on the saddle horn and spoke again in that soft, deep voice. "You're a quiet one. What's your name, son?"

Randy swallowed a dry lump in his throat, and finally found his voice. "Randall Abraham Zebediah Callum."

"I see," the stranger chuckled. "That's a lot of name for one boy. Suppose I just call you Mr. Callum?"

"Okay. What's your name, mister?"

"My name can't hold a candle to yours, so let's never mind."

"That's not fair. I told you mine."

"True enough," the man said, smiling. "I'm called Rule. Ulysses Rule."

"Don't you have a middle name?"

"No," Rule said. "I guess they gave all the good ones to you. You live here? What town is this?"

"Don't you even know where you are?" Randy said.

"I have come a long way, Mr. Callum. Through many

places that don't have names. I'm looking for a town called Bannon."

"Congratulations, you found it," Randy said. He leaned back and studied the stranger. "Funny, you don't look like a miner."

Rule chuckled. "No, I suppose not."

"No one comes here—hardly anyone—except from the mining company. What are you doing here?"

"One too many questions, Mr. Callum. You better run along now before you drown in the rain."

"I don't mind being wet. Why won't you tell me? It's a fair question, same as any man would ask you."

"Guess you got me again. There's a lot of backbone in you for one so young." Rule nodded thoughtfully. "I heard of a man living here," he said, "name of Tom McAllister. That sound familiar?"

"Sure. Everyone knows Mr. McAllister. He works at the mining company, along with most everyone else."

"Good," Rule said. His hand slid down and closed around a coil of rope hanging from the horn of his saddle. "He's my business."

Randy shook his head, not sure what the man was getting at. Then he glanced at the coiled rope in Rule's hand, and his breath caught in his throat.

It was a piece of craftsmanship, that rope, stout and well woven, so stiff it almost seemed to crackle. One part of it Randy couldn't stop staring at: the end tied off in a snug, spiraled noose. A kind of knot used for only one thing.

"That what I think it is?" Randy asked, embarrassed to hear the croak in his own voice.

Rule said, "Now you know."

"What's that got to do with Mr. McAllister?"

"That's between him and me. Private business. You understand?"

"It's a secret?"

"Just so. Can I trust you to keep this to yourself?"

Randy had never heard such a solemn secret before, much less had someone entrust him with it. "Yessir, mister," he said, as seriously as he could sound. "My sworn word on it."

"Good enough for me," Rule said with equal gravity. "I'll be needing a place to stay a few days, maybe a week."

"The hotel's full now, 'cause the mule train is in. But Mrs. Hardt has rooms at her boardinghouse. It's a big white place on the south end of the main street."

"Thank you, Mr. Callum." Rule drew the hood back around his face. "Maybe we'll meet again." He made a clicking noise low in his throat and the black horse strode away.

Randy watched him ride off and shook his head, wondering why it all felt like some strange dream. The rain and darkness seemed to gather around Rule. In moments he was gone, disappearing into the dark like a stone dropped into a lake.

After a moment, Randy remembered himself, turned away, and ran splashing through the mud for home. His clothes were soaked and he knew his mother would howl when she saw him. If Pa had beat him home, he might be in for a licking. But even that didn't seem to matter much now. His heart was pounding, his head dizzy with excitement. He could almost feel the secret like a hot coal smoldering in his head, trying to burn its way out. He prayed it wouldn't be long till he could share his big news . . . that a hangman had come to town.

CHAPTER 2

THE light at dawn was feeble and gray. After the night's rain the sky had turned clear, but it was fearsomely cold, and the sun looked pale and far away. Summer had barely come, it seemed, and already winter was snapping at the land, with hardly time between for leaves to fall.

Randy tumbled out of bed before first light, and his immediate thought was to wonder what the hangman would do that day. Since Randy had met Rule before anyone else, he thought of him as his own. He figured to stay close and keep an eye on him. Besides, if there was going be a genuine hanging, he didn't want to miss anything. Bannon was a quiet town and nothing half so interesting had ever happened there before.

He threw on his clothes in the dark. He sucked in his breath while pulling up his britches; his backside was still tender. His father had given him a licking that would raise welts on a buffalo. It had scared his parents pretty good when the storm hit and Randy couldn't be found.

Randy's father didn't whip him very often. Dan Callum and his wife considered themselves peace-loving folks—they didn't hold with fighting in any form or in any way causing other people harm. Randy was glad they thought that way, otherwise his backside would have been in a truly sorry state. During the lashing Randy's father kept saying, "This hurts me, son, much as it does you." If so, Randy thought, one had to marvel at how bravely his pa stood up to the hurt.

Anyway, since he had caused his parents so much bother last night, Randy decided to slip out without waking them.

No point in making them worry so early in the day. Besides, if they knew where he was headed, they might say no.

So he tiptoed out of the house. The cold air spiked his throat and he was so hungry it felt as if someone had taken a knife and cut his stomach clean away. Making him go to bed without supper had been his mother's idea of punishment, and it was a hard call whether that or the licking from Pa had caused him the most distress. He hated it when they teamed up on him that way.

He was careful of his bruises while he climbed over the fence. Then he took off for Mrs. Hardt's boardinghouse on the other end of town. He didn't come across another soul on the way; it was early and besides, it seemed to him people always lay abed a little longer the morning after a rain.

It was still fairly dark when he reached the boardinghouse, but a light was glowing in Mrs. Hardt's kitchen. The smell of frying bacon drifted out an open window, and Randy's stomach started growling so loud he feared it would give him away. He stood it for a couple minutes, then the cold and the smell of Mrs. Hardt's cooking made him decide on a change in tactics.

His mother oftentimes sold Mrs. Hardt bread and cakes, so Randy knew the old woman well and sometimes did small jobs for her. This seemed a perfect time to volunteer his services.

Mrs. Hardt answered the door without hesitation, despite the odd hour. "Why, Randall," she said. "What are you doing here? It's hardly even sunup yet."

Randy tipped his hat politely. "Morning, ma'am. Saw your light, so I knew you was up. I wondered if there was any jobs you needed done."

"Heavens, didn't you wake up with a full dose of ambition today? I don't know. . . . "

He looked past her and scanned the kitchen for inspiration. "Your woodbox 'ppears almost empty," he said quickly. "How about I haul in some wood for you?"

She scratched her chin in a thoughtful way. "I suppose you could. But what sort of wages do you expect, Randall?"

"Oh, you don't have to pay me. I just woke up early and didn't have nothing to do."

"That's very generous of you."

"Well, I guess I just woke up in a generous mood today." His stomach growled then, and he put his hands over it to muffle the sound.

"I see." Mrs. Hardt grinned, then stepped back and motioned him inside. "That would be fine, Randall. But I can't let you face strenuous work on an empty stomach. At least let me give you some breakfast."

Randy moved in eagerly. "Yeah. I mean . . . if you're sure that seems fair."

Her lined face broke into a wide smile. "Take a seat. Bacon and flapjacks sound all right?"

"Yes, ma'am!"

Randy sat down at the table she kept in the kitchen for her own meals. When she turned to the stove and started dishing up flapjacks, he resettled himself gingerly on the chair. Gritting his teeth, he had pretty much gotten used to the discomfort by the time she came back and set down a plate in front of him. With golden brown flapjacks and crispy bacon staring him in the face, he all but forgot the pain.

Randy attacked the food. Mrs. Hardt was probably the best cook in town—after his mother—and on that particular morning he decided it was probably more correctly a dead heat. He cleaned the plate in award-winning time, and she dished up the remaining bacon and flapjacks without even asking. Randy felt guilty, hogging food intended for her own breakfast, but she didn't seem to mind. She sat across from him, sipping coffee and smiling as if it pleased her just to watch him eat.

About midway through Randy's second helping, they heard the flooring creak overhead and knew her boarders were stirring. Mrs. Hardt jumped up and started in frying more food for her guests. It was a sight to see, the way she flew around that kitchen, all without seeming to hurry. Before he knew it, there were biscuits baking, eggs frying, and more flapjacks stacked high on a platter. There wasn't much Randy could do without getting in the way, so he stayed put and finished his meal at leisure. Last of all, she slapped venison steaks into the bacon grease, and the smell almost convinced Randy he was hungry all over again.

Somehow, she timed it all just right, and everything was ready by the time footsteps began thumping down the stairs. Mrs. Hardt loaded it all on a big trencher board and carried it out into the dining room. Randy slipped over to the door and eased it open a crack, so he could watch.

Two men were already at the table, and at that very moment, Rule came in from the hallway and dropped into a chair. His hair and beard were neatly combed, and he seemed wide-eyed and alert, as though he'd been up for hours already. He was still wearing that long wool cloak, even though it was warm inside the house. He didn't say much, just nodded his hellos to the others and helped himself to coffee.

One man was doing enough talking for all three of them anyway; he was a lanky young fellow of nineteen or twenty by the name of Johnson. Randy had seen him around town before, but hadn't known who he was before this. Johnson introduced himself as a cowhand in search of animals to tend. One day, he said, he had grown weary of the flatlands near Miles City, so had just left his job and started west, drawn by the mountains. He'd reached Bannon and the surrounding foothills by the time his money ran out. The easy way he joked with Mrs. Hardt and made himself to home suggested that he'd been a boarder with her a long time.

The other man was a stranger to Randy. He said his name was Nate Coleson, but offered little else. When Johnson pressed him, he allowed that he was from Kansas, and was looking for land to buy, with the idea of starting a cattle operation. Johnson got excited at this news, and the prospect of employment, but Coleson put him off, saying it would be a long time before he settled in Bannon, or anywhere. After that, Johnson concentrated on his meal in a disappointed, forlorn way.

To be fair, Mrs. Hardt's cooking merited a man's full attention—Randy's round, hard stomach could vouch for that. He watched Rule help himself to the flapjacks, eggs, biscuits, and homemade jams. To his surprise, though, Rule left the meat untouched.

Mrs. Hardt noticed it, too. "Not to your liking?" she asked.

Rule said, "I just don't care for any."

Johnson froze with the fork halfway to his mouth. "You what?"

"I could fry up some bacon, if you don't care for game," Mrs. Hardt said, fussing over Rule. "Or perhaps a beefsteak."

"No, thanks. I'm satisfied." Rule handed her his plate. She took it and sighed in a sad way, as if her feelings were hurt.

Before she could move off, Johnson grabbed her arm. "No sense to let good deer go to waste," he said, and slid Rule's venison onto his own plate. He cut off a chunk and chewed it quickly, as though afraid Rule might still change his mind. He glanced over at the hangman and shook his head in a puzzled way. "I never met a man before who could pass up a good cut of meat."

"Guess you can't say that anymore," Rule said.

Johnson couldn't let it go. He stared intently at Rule while chewing a bite that would choke a wolf. "I'd waste away if I was to eat like you. What keeps you standing?"

Rule ignored him, slid back his chair and stoked up an old Petersons pipe, puffing out clouds of blue smoke.

Mrs. Hardt cleared the table then. Randy rushed back to his chair when she carried the dishes into the kitchen. She seemed surprised to see him still there. "Did you get enough to eat, Randall?"

"Oh, yes, ma'am. Couldn't eat another bite. Sure was good, though." Then he blurted out what was on his mind. "Mrs. Hardt? What do you think of Mr. Rule? Seems a real interestin' gent, don't you think?"

"Why, how do you know him, Randall?" she asked.

"I met him last night, when he first rode into town. I was the one what sent him to stay here."

She smiled. "Is that so? I guess I'm beholden to you."

"But what do you think about him? Seems kinda different, wouldn't you say?"

"You haven't met many strangers before, have you?" She picked up a second pot of coffee from the stove and started back into the dining room. "I'll be back in a minute." She smiled and made a little toss with her head. "That woodbox still looks pretty empty from here."

She went back in with the second pot of coffee. Randy returned to his place at the door and peered out curiously.

This time Mrs. Hardt sat down with the men to share the coffee. Johnson packed chewing tobacco into his cheek and chatted with her while Rule smoked and Coleson sipped his coffee with the same full attention he had given his food.

After some idle gossip, Mrs. Hardt turned to bring Rule into the conversation. "We haven't seen so many new faces around these parts in ages. What brings you to Bannon?"

Rule puffed on his pipe a moment, then said gently, "It's private business, ma'am. No offense, but in a small place like this, a man has to guard his tongue."

Mrs. Hardt smiled and said, "We are a gossipy lot, that's true. Fact is, there's no such thing as a secret in Bannon. This is a company town, Mr. Rule. All peas in one small pod. And if one man noses into another's business, that's not maybe so bad, you see, because we're all in it together."

"The mining company?"

"That's right," Johnson said, breaking in. "*Silver*. Biggest damned strike you ever heard of."

Mrs. Hardt nodded. "Silver is the only thing that counts

here. Without it, this place wouldn't exist. Before they struck the lode, there weren't enough people in the territory to raise a barn. But now you see we got a pretty smart little town here. We're right happy with it, even if we did go in debt to our eyebrows to build it."

"How's that?"

"Investors, Mr. Rule. All of us. We put up a pretty penny for the right to settle here. They say it's a free country, but they darned well don't mean the cost of living in it."

At that, Coleson made a noise low in his throat, which might have been just congestion, but for him it passed for a laugh. "You got that right, lady," he muttered. They turned to him expectantly, but that was apparently all he had to say on the subject.

Rule looked back at Mrs. Hardt. "You mean the mining company charges you to live here?"

The elderly woman shook her head. "No, not exactly. Mr. Taggart doesn't charge us rent as such. But anyone who wants to live here pays a charge up front. It's a closed community, you see. I was skeptical at first. It didn't seem right, the mining company deciding what folks can stay and which can't. But all in all, it works to our mutual benefit. The town is growing steady, but without all the riffraff."

Rule nodded thoughtfully. "It does seem quiet. Not like any mining town I've been in before."

"It ain't like them others," Johnson said. "And the best part is, everyone has a stake in the company. The silver Taggart brings down from the hills is just as much ours as his."

"I don't know that I'd put it quite that way," Mrs. Hardt said gently. "But he's more or less correct. You see, Mr. Rule, we not only get the right to settle in Bannon, but a modest amount of stock in the company. So I guess you could say we are all in the mining business together."

"And profiting together?" Rule asked.

"We're not any of us exactly rich, not yet. But comfortable.

I'm doing as well as I ever did anywhere else. I aim to stay around a while."

"Me, too," Johnson added. "That is, if I can find work."

Rule stood up and nodded cordially to the old woman. "Mrs. Hardt, thank you for a fine meal and an interesting talk. But now I must see to my business. Can you tell me where to find the local lawman?"

Mrs. Hardt held a hand to her breast and took a deep breath before replying. "Heavens, I suppose that would be Will Murtry. We don't have a full-time sheriff, but Will gets a little money every month to keep the peace. It's a quiet town; not much happens but a brawl now and again when men get liquored up, or squabbling over this or that."

"Where do I find him?"

"He owns the feed store. Just head into town, you can't miss it. It would be hard to miss anything in this town, unless you were to work at it."

Rule nodded. "Thank you, ma'am." He swept his gaze over the two others. "Gentlemen."

"Hey," Johnson blurted, "if they need workers at the feed store, you'll let me know, okay?"

"I'll do that. But I doubt the matter will come up."

Johnson nodded glumly. "Yeah, guess so."

Coleson busied himself pouring more coffee, and didn't say a word when Rule brushed past him. All of them watched him as he headed for the door, and it was clear he knew it, but he hardly seemed to give it a thought.

Mrs. Hardt took the coffee cups into the kitchen, and frowned when she saw Randy throwing on his coat. "Thanks, ma'am," Randy said quickly. "That was good eatin'."

"Randall, my woodbox—"

But by then he had flung open the door and was gone.

CHAPTER 3

RULE stepped into the street, glanced around briefly, then started north into the center of town. Randy decided to meet up with him farther along, so as not to appear too obvious. His heart was thumping as he ran a parallel course behind two houses, then jogged back to intercept Rule in a way that would look accidental.

But when he came back out on the main street, Rule was farther along than expected. He was strolling casually, looking one way and then another as if interested by the size and shape of every building, but his long legs ate up ground. Randy had to run to catch up.

Rule didn't turn or even break stride when Randy pounded up behind him. "Morning, Mr. Callum. I was wondering when I would see you again."

Randy drew alongside and slowed to match pace. "How'd you know it was me?" he asked breathlessly. "You never even looked."

"I have eyes and ears. I believe in using them. Appears you were looking for me."

"You mind?"

"Not at all. Do your parents know you're here?"

"No," Randy admitted.

"I don't want you getting in trouble. Some folks don't like their boy hanging around strangers."

"I just want to talk. It don't seem wrong to be friendly, does it?"

"You always have an answer, don't you, Mr. Callum?"

Randy smiled. "My pa says that, too."

"I'm not surprised," Rule said.

"Where you going? I bet you're going to see Will Murtry. I'm right, ain't I?"

"Right as can be."

"It's all over town—about you being here, I mean. Bert Huffman came by our house last night and told my folks there was a stranger at Mrs. Hardt's boardinghouse. By now, I bet everybody knows about you."

"Is that a fact?" Rule shrugged.

"But I didn't say anything. I said I'd keep quiet, and I kept my word."

"Never thought you wouldn't. Appreciate it, all the same."

"I don't think they woulda believed me anyway," Randy added. They walked along quietly for a minute, and Randy noticed the way Rule stared at everything intently. "What's so interestin'? You looking for something?"

"Nice town here," Rule said. "Just getting a sense of it."

"Bannon? It's all right, I guess. But nothing much ever happens here. I can't wait to grow up and go somewhere far away."

"To people somewhere else, Bannon is *far away*. Ever think of that?"

"Yeah?"

"The place you grow up will always be a part of you. Do you think a man should be ashamed of where he comes from? Or should he be proud?"

"Proud, definitely."

"Good," Rule said. "Don't forget that."

"I still wish it was someplace more exciting, though."

"Well, that's all right. I guess I understand that."

"Is being a hangman something you're proud of?"

For a second Randy feared he'd said something wrong. Rule took a long time to reply. "It's a duty I feel bound to see done and done right," he said finally. "If it's carried out properly, responsibly, then I'm proud of that."

"So you'll be glad to lynch Mr. McAllister."

Rule stopped short and turned to face Randy. He put both

hands on the boy's shoulders and looked him square in the eyes. "Not at all," he said. "Any man's death is a sad thing. Especially a hanging. It means a man who could have done some good in this world went so wrong that we had to take his life away. That's about as sad as anything can be."

"I don't think Mr. Vickers would feel that way. I heard him say once he'd cheer and dance a jig the day he saw McAllister dead. He lost a lot of money to him one time at cards."

Rule scowled. "A man who could say something like that has more mouth than brains."

"I don't think he really meant it. I figure he was just talking big."

"I hope you're right, Mr. Callum." Rule started walking again. He pointed to a large square building with burlap sacks stacked on each side of the door. "That it?"

"Yes, sir. That's Murtry's feed store. S'pect you'll find him inside. He don't go out much."

"Well then, you better run along. My business with him could take a spell."

"I'd like to stay and listen, if it's all the same to you."

Rule shook his head. "That's not a good idea. This is private business, and there's a limit to how many secrets a friend should be burdened with."

"*Friend?* You mean that?"

"I said so, didn't I?" Rule smiled. "Thanks for seeing me here. It was nice of you to come make a stranger feel welcome."

"I don't mind. You don't talk to me the way other men do, like I'm still a kid."

"Not many folks talk straight to me either, Mr. Callum."

A little thrill shot down Randy's spine. No full-grown man had ever spoken to him so respectfully before. With all the dignity he could muster he said, "Well, I s'pose you better see about your business. I ought to go help my pa. He's probably wondering where I am."

Rule nodded. "Guess so. See you."

Randy waved, then walked away with head high. He felt as though everyone in town were watching him. He only wished it were so.

Rule turned and saw Murtry standing at the store's doorway to greet him. He was a big man with wide shoulders, a barrel chest, and a head as bald as a stone. For a moment they stared at each other, each sizing the other up. Then the sheriff chuckled. "Saw you comin'," he said. "Heard there was a stranger in town. My guess is that would be you."

"The name's Rule."

"Well, you're news, Rule. It was all over town by the time you pulled off your boots. Folks here would sell their first-born for a bit of gossip." He frowned and shook his head. "Can't get used to these people, never saw the like."

"You're not from around here, then?" Rule asked.

"Who is? Five years ago, there was nothing here. Then they found the vein. Silver has a way of bringing people together. Not always the best sort, though, if you take my meaning."

"The town seems pleasant enough."

Murtry stuck his head out and glanced up and down the street. There wasn't a soul to be seen in either direction. "They didn't exactly flock out to greet you, did they? Shut themselves up like you was carryin' plague or something."

"I didn't expect a parade," Rule said.

Murtry nodded. "Guess maybe you wouldn't." He stepped back and to one side. "Might as well come in and put your feet up."

Rule crossed to the chairs Murtry pointed to. The feed store was a large single room with shelves bowed under assorted weights and measures, scales, and crates of unknown contents. A counter ran the length of one wall, and nearly all the floor space was taken up by burlap sacks like those piled outside. A gritty film coated everything, as if a sandstorm had swept straight through the building; their boots kicked up dust and particles of grain.

Murtry went to a stove in the corner and poured some coffee into a dented tin mug. He glanced back at Rule. "You like some? I can find another cup here somewhere."

"No thanks," Rule said. He pulled out a knife and a plug of black tobacco and began shaving off a handful for his pipe.

Murtry looked at the tobacco enviously. "You have some of that to spare?" he asked.

"Help yourself." Rule held out his hand. Murtry broke off a large chunk and stuck it in his mouth. He wiped his lips and smiled, then hooked a chair with his toe and slid it across to Rule. He sat down on his own chair and kicked back, putting his boots up on the counter.

"Go on, make yourself to home." Murtry looked out the window while Rule seated himself. "I see folks are starting to wander back outside. S'pose they think I'll be jawin' at you a while. I have been known to speak a fair piece."

Rule dragged a match across the floorboards. Dust coated the match head and it took him two tries to get it lit. He held the flame over his pipe and puffed peacefully.

Murtry took aim at a bucket and spat a stream of brown juice. He nodded at Rule happily. "I gave up chewing, you know. My wife doesn't care for it."

"That so?"

"Yeah, I gave up chewing, to make her happy. Then she gave up *me*, for the same reason. She left about . . . " Murtry rocked back and stared at the ceiling as he calculated. "Oh, about three years ago now. You know, I'm beginning to think she's not coming back."

"Too bad. I'm sorry."

"Naw, don't be. I'm not." Murtry smiled. "Good tobacco."

Rule glanced around the dusty room and its squalor of neglect. He looked back to Murtry with a measured smile. "It's hard to believe a woman would leave all this."

The big man shrugged. "Don't blame her a bit. I'd leave in a minute, myself, someone was to make me the right offer."

"That's not exactly what I'm here for."

"Can't blame a man for trying," Murtry sighed. "I don't s'pose you came to buy some feed, neither?"

Rule shook his head. "Sorry."

"I didn't figure you for a stockman. You don't have the look, somehow. So, Mr. Rule, what exactly can I do for you?"

"I understand you represent the law here."

"That's a fact," Murtry said. "Not that it means much."

"I want you to arrest someone for me. You know a man named Tom McAllister?"

"Sure I know Tom. Arrest him, you say?"

"Big man, light hair, good-looking?"

"Sounds pretty close. But I don't know how good-looking he is. Has a scar across his right cheek about here." Murtry touched a finger to his face just below his right eye.

"That's him," Rule said. He leaned forward intently, and his knuckles grew white around his pipe.

Murtry's eyebrows crawled up his bald pate. "You don't seem altogether calm about this. You got something personal against Tom?"

"Yes. You could say that. If you want an honest answer."

"I don't have much use for the other kind," Murtry said. "Let's get down to straight talk. Just outta curiosity, what am I supposed to arrest him *for*? I know I'm just a part-time lawman in a two-bit town, but I know enough about the law not to arrest someone unless a crime's been committed."

"Treason and murder. Do those sound like crimes to you?"

"*Treason?* Mister, no one's confused me this much since my wife left. You got some explainin' to do."

Rule reached inside his cloak, brought out a rolled-up document, and tossed it on the counter in front of Murtry. "That will tell you all you need to know."

"I don't know what one piece of paper is gonna prove."

"Read it," Rule said.

Murtry glowered sullenly and pulled a pair of spectacles from his shirt pocket. He slipped them on and grumbled under his breath, as if ashamed by his poor vision. Rocking back on his chair, he unrolled the page and held it up to the light.

A second later, his chair crashed back to the floor. Murtry yanked off his spectacles and shook his head. "Is this thing genuine? This is an order signed by the president himself."

"Is that authority enough for you?"

"I never saw such a thing. I don't know whether I believe it or not."

"That is a presidential commission, granting me the legal authority to track down all the men on that list, and to personally carry out their executions. You'll find McAllister's name included."

Murtry nodded. "I see it. *Execute* him? This is the damnedest thing I ever heard of. What did Tom McAllister do to make the president of the United States sign something like this?"

"It's a long story from a long time ago."

"Then you can start right now," Murtry said. He looked around with a sad expression. "I'm not going anywhere."

CHAPTER 4

RULE didn't seem in any big hurry to get on with his story; he tamped his pipe leisurely until it was drawing to his satisfaction, and stared past Murtry at a point on the wall, as if he could see the memory nailed up there like a painting. His voice was soft, but once he began, it took on an edge and became bitter, harsh. The words came slowly, as though dredged out by considerable effort. His eyes became cool and distant.

"It goes back to the war," he said. "That's when I met McAllister—we were in the same outfit. It was a bad time. We were fighting a winner's war, but earning only a standoff. Stalemate. No ground won or lost. But the killing still went on. Every day we lost more men. Some died of camp sickness, from bad food or a lack of food; a lot just had all they could take and ran off. It seemed the stalemate would last forever, longer than we could. Then came Whiteridge."

"Can't say I ever heard of it," Murtry said. "That a place, is it?"

Rule nodded grimly. "Just a smudge on the map, nowhere special. A nothing little town on the Mississippi River. The people there didn't care beans about the war. They would lean pro-South one day, pro-North the next, whichever way the wind blew. It didn't matter to them that good men were fighting and dying—the war for them was a chance to get rich—and they weren't about to let conscience stand in their way."

"How's that?"

"Whiteridge was a town of river rats, pilots and bargemen dealing in contraband. Trading between the two armies."

24

"The war didn't do much to stop business, sure enough," Murtry said. "I heard tell of more than one man who got rich supplying both sides."

Rule nodded and paused to strike another match. But he didn't raise the flame to his pipe, just sat with his pipe in one hand and the burning match in the other as though he had forgotten about them both.

"There's just no end to what some folks will do in their own behalf," Murtry prompted, after a moment.

Rule stirred, stared at the flame burning down the match toward his fingers. He shook it out, sighed, and started again. "They were dealing in salt. The South needed salt desperately, to preserve meat for the troops. A bag of it would sell for almost seventy-five dollars."

Murtry let out a soft whistle. "I can see why they was tempted some."

"What the greedy bastards usually did was take their money from the salt transaction and buy up Southern cotton, then ship that back North. Buy it at twenty cents a pound, sell it for sixty cents to a dollar. So they made money going both ways, lots of it. No way any government, or even a war, could stop trade when there was that kind of money to be made."

"Where does McAllister fit in to all this?" Murtry asked.

"I'm getting to that," Rule said. "He was one of the profiteers. The merchants had spies working for them on both sides. When you smuggle cargo through the middle of a war, it helps to know where the two armies are located, where they're headed next, and most of all, where the next battle's going to be. Those river rats had a better picture of how the war was shaping up than any soldier in the lines. They knew our plans as if they had a front seat in the general's planning sessions.

"Still, the fighting was a major *inconvenience* for them. They avoided most of the fighting pretty handily, but the war kept coming closer and closer, making it harder and more risky to slip their shipments through. The two armies started converging near Whiteridge; a battle was forming practically on top of them, and the traders didn't care for that. They decided it was time to take action of their own. Like it or not, they had to choose sides."

"Hell, why'd they have to favor one or the other, if they was making money from both?" Murtry asked.

"The stalemate couldn't last forever. One side or the other had to come out on top. The traders decided to make sure it was the one they favored. So they took steps to tip the scales toward the South."

"Why'd they pick the Rebs?"

"The South needed goods more badly, so the traders got a better price from them. From their point of view, it was no contest."

Murtry rubbed the top of his bald head so hard, if he'd had any hair left, it would have rubbed clean off. "Took *steps,* you said? Meanin' what, exactly?"

Rule's pipe had grown cold. He set it down and took a deep breath before starting in again. "They began dealing in a different sort of commodity—*casualties.* They offered commissions to their spies within the Northern ranks, extra pay to any who could help steer Federals into Rebel traps. A bonus for each dead Yankee.

"Just at that time the stalemate was ending. For the first time in months, we won new ground. The Rebs were retreating, and the front moved within a few miles of Whiteridge. Our outfit was given orders to move south down the river and occupy the town, make sure the Rebs couldn't use it to bring up troops in a flanking movement."

"And the traders knew you Yanks were coming?"

Rule nodded grimly. "They knew. McAllister was one of half a dozen spies living and sleeping right among us, sharing our food, laughing at our jokes . . . and secretly plotting to profit from our deaths."

Murtry shook his head. "Seems hard to believe McAllister

could do a thing like that. To tell the truth, I always sort of liked him."

"We all liked him, too," Rule said bitterly. "But he betrayed us for a chance to line his pockets."

"So what happened?" Murtry asked.

"Fifty of us headed downriver to occupy Whiteridge. McAllister scouted up ahead and spotted a barge moving downstream, said he'd talked the captain into carrying us. The notion of floating along peaceful and easy instead of slogging through mud sounded like heaven. We boarded the barge and settled down on deck. The cargo was piles of heavy sacks, almost like pillows —perfect for stretching out and drowsing in the sun. We hardly gave a thought to what was in those sacks. It was salt, tons of contraband salt, and the barge was manned by smugglers.

"It was the most quiet, relaxing time we'd had in months. By the time we neared Whiteridge, most of the men were asleep. Just as we pulled up to the dock, McAllister and five others slipped overboard and waded ashore. The barge crew went with them."

Murtry scowled and spit more tobacco juice into the bucket. "So they slunk off like rats, did they? Just in time to save themselves."

Rule nodded. "It was a near perfect trap. The lieutenant shook us all awake and we lined up on deck, waiting to march off once the boat was tied off. But then the barge crew reappeared on shore. There was a big warehouse right next to the dock; they swung open the doors, then ran back into the woods. Inside that warehouse was what looked like a whole division of Rebs."

"Holy days!" Murtry gasped.

"There we were, all lined up, still rubbing sleep from our eyes, and suddenly we were staring down the barrels of a hundred rifles."

Murtry rubbed his bald pate to a polished shine. "Case like

that," he muttered, "I'd of surrendered so fast, it woulda made your head spin."

"They didn't give us a chance," Rule said. "Taking prisoners was not part of their plans. Thirty men fell in the first barrage. It wasn't even good target practice for them. We were so bunched up, they could hardly miss. In just seconds, there wasn't a living soul on that boat."

"They killed *everyone*?"

"Out of forty-four men, only one lived to give witness against the traitors. Just one."

Murtry stared at Rule. "You?"

Rule nodded. "In the first seconds I was hit three times. The force of the bullets blew me clear off the boat. That's all that saved my life. I dragged up on shore a few yards downstream, lay under a fallen tree, certain I would never get up again. But I was lucky. No bullet struck bone, all went through clean. I didn't know that then; I thought I was dying, and maybe I was. What I saw the rest of that day made me almost wish I had.

"The Rebs hauled all the bodies off the boat, tossed them together in a big pile on shore. Then they threw lamp oil on the pile and set it afire."

"Why didn't they just toss the bodies in the river?" Murtry asked.

Rule shrugged. "Maybe they didn't want bodies bobbing up at unexpected places downstream. Maybe they were sickened by what they'd done, and wanted to burn the evidence clean away. Who knows what went through their heads?"

"And you had to sit there and watch it all?"

"All day, waiting to die," Rule said. "The sight of those burning bodies, the smell . . . I almost prayed I would die. Until later, when I saw something else, something that gave me reason to live."

"What's that?" Murtry asked softly.

"I saw the traitors receive their payoff. McAllister and his henchmen. I swore a promise to myself that if I lived I would see them pay for their treachery."

Murtry didn't speak for a long moment. He swore something soft and below hearing, then said, "McAllister was really one of them? You sure of that?"

"Do you think, after that experience, I could ever forget any of their names or faces?"

"No, I s'pose not."

"I've been after those six men since the day the war ended," Rule said. "The president granted me this authorization, and his personal wishes for success."

"War's been over for years. A mighty long time to stay angry."

Rule shook his head. "It's not hard to do."

Murtry spit in the bucket once more. He stared out the window blankly as he considered that. Finally, he turned back to Rule and shrugged. "I don't know whether to believe any of this or not. You could be what you say you are, and that document looks real enough. But how can I be sure? I can't let you hang Tom without I'm real certain it's the right thing to do."

"What would it take to convince you?" Rule asked.

"Give me a week. I'll send word to the federal marshals. If they notify me it's proper for you to string up Tom McAllister, then he's all yours and good riddance. But if they say they never heard of Ulysses Rule and this-here presidential order, then I'm gonna be very upset with you, Mr. Hangman."

"Fair enough."

"You don't mind waiting that time?"

"I've been after McAllister for years. I can wait a week."

Murtry nodded. "So what happens now?"

"You arrest McAllister."

"Figured you might say something like that." Murtry went behind the counter and pulled some handcuffs and a set of keys from inside a drawer. "I bet you can even tell me what charge I'm to arrest him for."

"Say you're just going to hold him on suspicion, if you like. I'm willing to wait on your confirmation from the marshals, but I guarantee you McAllister won't be. The moment he learns that I'm here, he's going to cut out and never come back."

Murtry started for the door and motioned for Rule to follow. "Then I guess we better go. Considerin' the way people talk, I'll be surprised if he ain't heard already."

Rule got to his feet quickly. "You don't mind me tagging along?"

"Hell, *someone's* got to explain the situation. I don't know if I believe it enough to convince myself, much less make McAllister take us serious."

"He will," Rule said. "Believe me, he will."

Murtry stopped in the door and held up his hand. "No offense, but I got a queasy feeling in my gut. Seems to me a man in your line of work might pack a little persuasion. You got a gun somewhere beneath that robe of yours?"

Rule nodded.

"Leave it here. I don't want you getting any sudden ideas once you see him."

"A wise precaution," Rule said. "You make a pretty good sheriff for a part-timer." His right hand dipped inside his cloak. In one smooth motion a sawed-off shotgun appeared from nowhere.

Murtry's eyes grew round. "That's some mean-looking little gun you got there."

"It serves its purpose." Rule unclipped the Greener from its sling and set it on the countertop. Then he pulled a long-barreled revolver from the holster at his waist and set it down as well. Raising his left arm, he pulled up the sleeve and revealed a small double-barreled derringer in a leather wrist holster.

"You're a damned walking arsenal. What else you got hid on you?"

"That's all."

"All right, then." Murtry shrugged into his coat, then grabbed a battered felt hat and jammed it down over his shiny bald head. From a notched wall cabinet, he took an old .50 Sharps rifle and rested it in the crook of his arm. "Let's go get it over with."

CHAPTER 5

RANDY'S backside was sore from all the sitting around, waiting for Rule and the sheriff to show themselves. He had never expected them to talk so long. His patience was nearly all used up when, finally, Rule and Murtry stepped out into the street. Randy's heartbeat quickened when he saw the rifle in Murtry's arms. He let them have a good head start, then followed after them, eager to see what would happen next.

Murtry and Rule walked along as if on a Sunday stroll. People stared at them through windows, and others drifted outside, drawn by the unusual sight. It was odd enough, just seeing Murtry outside his store during daylight hours, much less walking alongside a total stranger, and the rifle was a sure sign something was up.

Randy cut behind the blacksmith's shop, hoping to make up time by angling across town. Mr. Larson was at work out in front of his forge, crouched over with the hoof of a bay mare clamped between his legs. He was pounding a shoe onto the mare's hoof when Randy came running past and spooked the horse so that it reared back and threw the shoe. It smacked against the shop wall like a cannonball. The blacksmith shook his hammer at Randy and yelled something in Swedish. It sounded like gibberish, but Randy got his meaning clear enough.

Once past the blacksmith's, Randy ran into his best friend in the whole town, a miner's son name of Bill Kitson. Bill was playing by the schoolyard with some shingle darts, wood shingles shaved down into sharp triangles, with a little notch at the nose, where a knot on the end of a string catches. The string is snapped like a whip, and the dart shoots off like an arrow. Bill was flinging his darts at a circle he'd marked on the ground some thirty yards away. That was a pretty good fling, but then Bill was the best at darts Randy knew of, and he was rightly proud of the fact, too.

He saw Randy coming and cocked back his arm for another toss. "Hey, watch this," he said. "Betcha this one's right in the bull's-eye, for sure."

"I got no time for that now," Randy said, without slowing a whit. "This is no day for kids' games."

Bill frowned and started to complain, but saw something in Randy's urgency, dropped his darts, and right away fell in step beside him. "Hey, where ya goin'?" he asked. "And why ya walkin' so stifflike?"

"Big things happening," Randy said breathlessly. "Murtry's gonna arrest Tom McAllister."

"Naw, you're joshin' me. C'mon, what would he go and do that for?"

"It's true, I tell you. He's on his way now, and he's packing his rifle."

"Gosh, no foolin'?" Bill's eyes opened big as saucers. "What did Mr. Mac do to get hisself arrested for?"

"Can't tell you," Randy said smugly. "Private business."

"That means you don't know, huh?"

"Do too."

"You do not," Bill said. "You're pullin' my leg about the whole thing, aren't ya?"

"It's a secret is all, and I can't tell you. Shut up and come on or we'll miss all the action."

"I'm comin', I'm comin'," Bill said. "You're the one slowin' us down. Still think you're joshin' me, though. Mr. Mac ain't the sort to get hisself arrested, unless it's just to sleep off a drunk, and my pa says that ain't no crime at all, it's just a fact of nature."

"Getting drunk is a fact of your pa's nature, maybe. This ain't nothing like that."

Bill looked away quickly. Randy regretted what he'd said. It was true Bill's father took a drink or three too many, all too often, but that was no more than most miners did. Anyway, it wasn't Bill's fault his father was a drunk. "Sorry," Randy mumbled.

Bill nodded and let it go. Randy supposed his friend was used to hearing his father badmouthed and didn't need much apology to be satisfied.

The Taggart Mining and Development Company was on the very edge of town, set back on a little cross street that had no real name, but everybody called it Silver Lane. The office was the grandest building in town, a three-story frame house painted white with bright stripes of red trim every few feet. Folks joked that if you looked at the place at night, while the stars were out, you'd think you were looking at the biggest American flag anyone ever dreamed of. Randy had come by one night once, to see for himself, and all it looked like was an ordinary big house in the dark.

Randy and Bill heard the noise of the crowd even before they turned the corner onto Silver Lane. Rule and Murtry had just come to a stop outside the mining office, and there were at least twenty people tailing them. The crowd was milling around, chattering and trying to guess what was up, making a racket that alerted the men inside. Taggart and a couple of his teamsters appeared at the windows, looking out with round eyes. Randy would have given up his newly won nickel just to know what was going through their heads at the sight of all those people.

"That the stranger with Murtry?" Bill whispered. "You didn't tell me he was part of this."

"Mr. Rule," Randy said. "His name's Rule."

"How you know that? Who said so?"

"He told me so, himself," Randy said proudly. "When I met him."

Bill squinted at him sideways. "Aw, go on. You did not."

"Did so. I was the first person in town to have words with him. We're friends now, him and me."

"Fibber. Tell me another."

Randy said solemnly, "Hush, Murtry's fixin' to talk."

The sheriff turned around slowly and deliberately and glared the whole crowd into silence. The look on his face made a few people at the front push back a couple steps. "Don't you folks have any business of your own?" he barked. "This don't concern you. Go on back home, and leave us to do what we come for."

"What did you come for, Murt?" somebody yelled out. "What's going on?"

A mutter went through the crowd, as a dozen voices echoed the question. "Yeah, tell us."

"What'cha doing, Murt? Gonna foreclose on Mr. Taggart?" Everybody laughed at that one. The sheriff frowned and raised his hand for quiet. But just when the muttering died off, someone called out, "Hey, Murt! Who's that with you?"

Murtry glanced over at Rule, shook his head, and looked back at the crowd. "You'll know what you need to know soon enough, but not until I'm ready to tell you. So all of you back off and give a man some room to breathe."

Nobody moved.

Murtry scowled. "This is official business," he grumbled. "I'm ordering you to break it up and go back home before I take a mind to arrest the whole lot of you."

Nobody minded that command either, though one or two people chuckled. Murtry turned back to Rule and shrugged. "See what I told you?"

"You do have a way with them," Rule said.

Just then, the door to the mining office swung open and Taggart stepped out. The crowd got quiet all of a sudden, without any prompting. Alongside Taggart were two of his teamsters, Greene and Younger. They were big, brutish men with meaty faces and shoulders like oxen, but neither seemed all that impressive while standing next to Taggart.

The boss man stepped out to the edge of the porch, stared at the crowd in a bored way, as if such gatherings were a common occurrence.

"Morning, Sheriff," Taggart said. He motioned at Murtry's rifle. "Going hunting, are you?"

"You might say that. Hunting of a sort, maybe."

"Brought plenty of help with you."

"They're not part of this," Murtry said, tipping his head toward the crowd. "Folks can't seem to mind their own business."

"I'm a busy man, Sheriff. What is it you want?"

"Would you ask Tom McAllister to step outside, sir? We need to speak with him."

"We?" Taggart swiveled his gaze over to Rule. "Who's this? I don't know you, do I?"

Rule said, "I don't know you, either."

"It's clear you're not from around here," Taggart said, puffing out his chest like a proud turkey. "Everyone in these parts knows James Johnson Taggart."

"Like you say, I'm not from around here. If I was, maybe I'd be more impressed."

Taggart's smile hardened. Murtry stepped between them. "We can do the introductions once you bring out Tom. Sorry, but I have to insist. Call him out now. Please, sir, or we'll have to go in and get him."

Taggart frowned. "Nobody steps inside my place uninvited. You're kinda forgetting yourself, aren't you, Murtry?"

"This is a sheriffin' matter," Murtry said quietly. "We come for Tom . . . we mean to take him with us."

"What! You lost your mind?" Taggart glared at Rule. "You the one put him up to this?"

"I suggest you hear him out," Rule said.

"Oh, you do, do you?" Taggart's face was turning red to match the stripes on his building. He glanced over his shoulder at Younger. "Get Tom out here," he ordered. "Go on.

We'll put an end to this foolishness." The teamster disappeared back inside the office.

"Wow, what do you s'pose they want with Mr. Mac?" Bill said to Randy. "You think he coulda done something wrong?"

"You'll see," Randy said, trying not to sound too pleased with himself.

Then everybody got quiet all at once, as Younger came back through the doorway, and right behind him was Tom McAllister. When he saw the crowd McAllister's eyes opened wide and he played a finger across his scar in a self-conscious way. "What's going on here?" he asked Taggart. "You wanted to see me about something?"

"Not me," Taggart said. "These two soft-brains here claim they got business with you." He pointed to Murtry and Rule.

Taggart stilled the crowd with the faintest wave of his hand. He looked at Murtry and spoke so his voice carried to every man there, as if he were a politician asking for their vote. "Now, Sheriff. Suppose you tell us what this is all about?"

Murtry ignored him, turned calmly to Rule. "Well? Is this the man you been looking for?"

Rule gave a short nod of his head. His eyes had turned cold, and his face was clamped up in the tightest frown Randy had ever seen on a man.

Murtry sighed and stepped up in front of McAllister. "Tom, you need to come with us. As representative of the law in this town, I'm arresting you on suspicion of serious crimes. You will be held in custody until conclusion of a formal investigation into the allegations against you. Federal marshals are being notified of this action, and we expect word back from them soon."

McAllister exploded. "Murtry, your head been baking in the sun too long? What the devil are you going on about?"

"I mean what I say," Murtry said softly. "It would be best for everyone if you come along quietly."

Taggart pushed up boldly. "Now, see here—"

"This don't concern you, sir," Murtry said. "I'll ask you to keep out of it."

"What allegations?" McAllister asked. "Who says I ever committed any crimes?"

"I do," Rule said.

"And who the hell are you?"

Taggart pounded his fist against the porch rail. "This is outrageous. Mister, you'd better think twice before mouthing slanderous talk to a friend of mine. I'll run you out of town personally. Murtry, you want to keep your job, you stop this nonsense. I don't know what stories this stranger's filled your empty head with, but you mind now, and do as I say."

Murtry glared back and spoke in a carefully controlled voice. "Whether I keep bein' sheriff or not, I am sheriff now, and I'm gonna do the job. We come to arrest Tom McAllister, and I don't reckon to leave without him."

The porch flooring gave out a loud squeal as the two burly teamsters started forward, their fists raised. Murtry turned casually, and the Sharps, still nestled in his arm, swung to bear on them. He didn't cock the rifle, or make any effort to aim it, but the cannonlike muzzle of that weapon was enough to make the men stop dead still.

The sheriff nodded toward two chairs at the far end of the porch. "Those seats look soft enough to me. You two plant your butts on them for a spell. No reason to stir yourself."

"Just as you say, Sheriff," the one called Greene grumbled. He screwed up his face in thought for a minute, then slowly raised his hands.

"Ol' Greenie here's got the idea," Murtry said. "He caught on right fast. Younger, why don't you follow his lead?"

Swearing bitterly, the other man lifted his hands.

"See now, this ain't goin' so bad. I think we're all doing just fine."

Taggart raged, "You dumb Irish bastard. What the hell are you playing at?" He slipped a hand inside his coat as if reaching for something.

Before anyone else realized what was happening, Rule dipped a hand into his boot top and lunged forward. A knife appeared in his hand as though from nowhere. With his free hand he grabbed Taggart's hair and pulled down until the big man's throat rested on the tip of the upturned dagger.

Rule said, "Suppose you open that coat—real slow, and let us all see what it is you're so eager to get hold of."

Taggart glared back at Rule. "I was just getting a cigar."

"That so? Then you won't mind showing it to us."

"Mister, you're making a bad mistake." Taggart's head bobbled as he spoke, and a tiny bead of blood sprouted on the underside of his chin. He undid the buttons of his coat, eased it open, and pulled a long black cigar from the inside breast pocket. "See?"

Rule reached out and yanked Taggart's coat open all the way. Resting in his belt was a Colt revolver. Rule lifted it out and pointed it at Taggart's cigar. "I suppose this is what you light it with?"

"I forgot that was even there."

"Careless of you," Rule said. "You won't mind if we borrow it for a spell, since it means so little to you." He tossed the gun gently to Murtry, who caught it one-handed, without moving his rifle off the teamsters on the porch chairs.

Murtry said to Rule, "Seems to me we're wearing out our welcome here. If it's all the same to you, I'd as soon say our good-byes now."

"Suits me," Rule said. He crossed behind McAllister and gave him a nudge in the back. McAllister glared at Rule and blinked in confusion. "Who the hell are you?" he said again.

"Take a good look," Rule said. "Think back."

"Mister, I don't know you from Adam."

Rule's voice was choked with anger. "You remember these names? Jeffers, Cantry, Latham, Smith, Talbert, Meeks . . ."

"I'll be damned," McAllister muttered. He stared at Rule, and his eyes opened wide. "Rule? Ulysses Rule."

"So you do remember."

"I thought you was dead."

"I nearly was, thanks to you and the others."

"You got it wrong. I don't know what you think happened, but you got to believe me—"

Rule shook his head. "I was there. I saw it all, just twenty paces from where you stood."

"You couldn't," McAllister sputtered. "There was no one but us and—" He bit off the last words with clicking teeth and a sudden intake of breath.

Murtry said, "Go on. I'm finding this real interesting."

"Never mind," McAllister grumbled. "Forget it."

"No one but you and a pile of corpses," Rule said. "That's what you were going to say, wasn't it?"

"I don't remember."

"I do," Rule said. "I'll never forget a moment of it. Or a single one of you who sold us out. How much did they pay you, McAllister? I've always wondered what price you put on the lives of those young men."

"Go to hell," McAllister snapped.

Rule reached a hand inside his cloak. Murtry gave him a sharp glance. "You better not be thinkin' of doing anything rash."

"Just this," Rule said, and drew out the document. He uncurled the paper and held it up for McAllister to read. "See this? This is an order of execution signed by the president of the United States. Your execution, McAllister. That's what I'm here for."

McAllister began to tremble. "You're insane! I never . . . Murtry, you're not going to listen to him, are you?"

The bald man shrugged. "That's a mighty official-looking piece of paper."

"You can't do this to me. You lost your minds, both of you."

"Well, now," Murtry said casually. "I don't see how insulting me is going to help your cause much."

McAllister gulped deep drafts of air, calming himself.

"You're the sheriff. I'm in your custody; you're responsible for me. You're not going to let this lunatic do anything crazy, are you?"

"Steady down, boy. I'm not decided what way it's going to happen yet. That depends on the federal authorities. We'll have word back from them by the end of the week, and then we'll know whether you go with them or to the hangman here."

"Hangman?" McAllister choked on the word. He stared at Rule. "You?"

"In my room there's a fine new rope waiting for you, McAllister. It's strong and well made, without an inch of play. The end will be short and painless. I promise you that."

"You got no right to threaten me. You're no hangman."

"That's my business now," Rule said. "I learned it well over the last few years. Braun and Logan and Sharpe all had their turn before you."

McAllister hissed, "You lynched Marty Logan and Bill Sharpe?"

"And Braun," Rule reminded him. "The six of you went different ways after the war. It's been a long chore tracking so many separate trails. Tim Rivers died in Arizona; his horse threw him down a ravine. That left five. After you, there'll be only one."

"What kind of man are you?

Rule turned his back on him and motioned to the sheriff. "All right, let's go."

Murtry nodded. Rule reached out to grab McAllister's arm, but McAllister flinched and drew away from him.

"You keep him off me, Murtry. You got that? Keep this son of a bitch out of my sight. Or so help me, you'll regret it."

Murtry shrugged. "It don't seem to me like you're in any position to be making threats."

McAllister looked back at Taggart over his shoulder. "You can't let them get away with this. Aren't you gonna do anything to stop them?"

"I am thinking on it," Taggart said slowly. "Boys, how do you feel about it?" He glanced over at his henchmen, and the two bruisers got to their feet. Greene started slowly rolling up his sleeves.

Murtry shook his head sadly. "Mr. Taggart, you better tell your monkeys to grab themselves some chair again. Otherwise, you're going to lose them. This Sharps will put a bullet clean through both of them at once, and never stop till it passes through the wall and out the other side for least half a mile."

"You're bluffing," Taggart growled.

Murtry leveled the gun at Greene's chest. The muzzle pointed to his heart, steady and unwavering. "Nope, I never was any good at bluffing. Just never got the knack of it."

"You're through in this town, Murtry. So help me."

"I heard some threats in my time. That one don't sound so bad. Anyway, it's your decision, Mr. Taggart. You tell them to sit down and stay out of it. Otherwise, you're gonna be short two hired monkeys and I'll arrest you for interfering with an officer of the law in the course of his rightful duty. Or we can all part company peaceablelike. Your call. One way or another, it's all the same to me. But I mean what I say."

Taggart and Murtry locked eyes for a long moment, then Taggart blinked and waved a hand shortly. "All right, boys. Back off. Let 'em go."

The two teamsters looked at each other with expressions of relief.

"Wise choice, Mr. Taggart," Murtry said. "I knew I could count on you to act sensible. You got any questions, you know where to find me."

"I sure do," Taggart growled. "You bet I do."

Murtry steered McAllister off through the crowd. People backed away as if they were marked with the pox.

McAllister scowled and spat in the dusty street. "You two are a bad joke. You can't lock me up. There's no jail in this town; where do you think you're gonna keep me?"

"Don't you worry none about it," Murtry said. "I got just the place, and you're gonna like it fine. I even turned over the lice to air out on their bottom sides."

Bill turned to Randy and he was practically squirming with excitement. "Gosh, did you see that?" he said.

"Who else do you think it was standing right beside you?" Randy said. "It happened just like I told you it would."

"It sure did. Did you see the way Murtry stood up to 'em? He even talked back to Mr. Taggart. I never figured him for a man with so much backbone."

"Could be Rule had something to do with that," Randy suggested.

Bill shook his head in a dreamy way. "I can't hardly believe it. A real criminal living amongst us all this time, and we never once suspected."

"He ain't a for-real criminal just yet. They only took him on suspicion. They still got to prove to the marshals that he's guilty and deserves to hang."

"You know, I never did like McAllister much, come to think on it," Bill said. "He always seemed kinda shifty-eyed and shady to me."

Randy screwed up his face to show Bill what he thought of such talk. "Oh, sure. You never. You wouldn't know a criminal if he was standing right in front of you."

"I dunno," Bill said, and his face broke into a big silly grin. "I know the look of a fella in trouble pretty well. I get lots of practice by lookin' at you."

"What's that s'posed to mean?"

Bill grinned even bigger, took Randy by the arm, and turned him half around. "Look over there," he said. "Here comes your pa."

Sure enough, Dan Callum was storming down the street with a full head of steam, pushing through the crowd as though he hardly noticed they were there.

Bill leaned over and whispered in Randy's ear, "He was lookin' for you earlier. Said you run off this morning without a word to no one, and him with a full day's work planned for you, too. He was powerful upset. Sure glad it wasn't me he was after."

"Thanks a lot," Randy growled. "Why didn't you say nothing before this?"

"You the one did the running off," Bill said. "I figured you knew about it already."

Callum yelled out then, "You and I are gonna have words, son. I'll teach you not to go runnin' off on me." He kept charging on, and the closer he came the more nervous Randy got. The boy looked around, wondering if there was still time to make a break for it.

But Bill's hand clamped down on his arm even tighter. "Don't even think it," he said.

"Some friend you are. What'cha think you're doing?"

"He'd be mad at me, too, if I was to let you go now. You're just gonna have to stay and take your medicine." And his fingers cinched around Randy's arm so hard it nearly cut off the blood.

Randy sighed and hung his head in defeat. The hand of friendship could be a powerful hard thing to tolerate, sometimes

CHAPTER 6

IT seemed to Randy that sundown would never come. His father was determined to finish building the new Union Hall, and seemed bound to work Randy till he dropped. By the time they drove the last nail it was almost too dark to see the nose on your own face, and by then Randy was too tired to even raise his hand and search for it, if the need had arisen. Callum stepped back to admire the job, put his arm around the boy's shoulders, and said, "I'm proud of you, son. You put in a good day's work, even if we did start off on the wrong foot."

Randy swelled up with pride, and there was a lump in his throat of pure shame over the way he'd acted, because he knew it hurt his father when he had to be strict. His pa was a gentle man; there wasn't a drop of meanness in his nature even though he lived in a hard place and time which had soured many a man of kindly disposition.

For years Dan Callum had worked in the mines alongside some of the roughest, most wild-spirited men anywhere, and got along with them as well as with cultured bankers and businessmen. The miners were a rowdy lot who didn't respect a man till he'd proved himself with his fists, but Callum never raised a hand against anyone. The times someone crossed him or tried to take advantage of his gentle ways, he would challenge the man to a duel—with pickaxes. They'd enter a contest to see who could chip the most stone, and Callum would slave away till his opponent fell from sheer exhaustion. Many a man said afterwards a whupping was easier than the torture of matching Callum at work. There was hardly anyone his equal at hammers or pickaxes.

A son can be proud of a father like that, so it shamed Randy the times he gave his pa cause for disappointment. This time, though, he was too tired to dwell on his shame; he was just grateful the day was over and they could finally go home. But that's when the other shoe dropped.

Callum slapped his son gently on the back, then said, "I'll gather the tools and clean up here. You go on now and finish up the rest of your chores."

Randy's jaw dropped. "What other chores?" he groaned.

"Mrs. Hardt tells me you promised to fill her woodbox. So you best get along over there. It won't happen by itself."

"Now? I'm so done in I can hardly—"

Callum glanced at Randy over his shoulder and the boy swallowed the rest of his protest in a quick gulp. "You gave your word, and a man's word has to count for something. Don't cheapen it with promises you don't mean to keep."

"Yessir," Randy mumbled. He knew when his father started making statements like that, there was no way to change his mind. So he turned and started dragging his aching body in the direction of the boardinghouse.

"Don't worry, son. Your supper will keep," Callum called after him. "You'll feel better once this is done. You'll see."

Randy didn't bother to answer. He knew his father was right. But feeling good about a job once it's done is small comfort while the job is yet to be done.

It was a long walk to the boardinghouse. The night was getting cold, and every muscle in Randy's body was stiff and sore.

He was so weary, in fact, that it wasn't until he saw the light glowing in the window of Mrs. Hardt's sitting room, that he remembered Rule was staying there. His spirits picked up a notch at the notion of seeing him again; after the events that morning Rule and McAllister were all anyone could talk about. It was like knowing somebody famous, and Randy felt a little taller remembering that the man everyone was so curious about had called him his friend.

He went in the kitchen door, but didn't see Mrs. Hardt anywhere, so wandered into the sitting room. It was a cozy place with a fire blazing in a huge rough stone hearth. Mrs. Hardt was in a rocking chair by the fire with a pile of sewing in her lap. Rule sat across from her, and he was reading a subscription book by Dickens, *Great Expectations*. Randy held his hat in his hands and walked up to the old lady with head bowed, like a contrite sinner come forward to give witness at a prayer meeting.

"Evening, Mrs. Hardt, Mr. Rule. Hope I ain't interruptin' nothing."

She put her sewing aside and looked up with a warm smile. "Why, good evening, Randall. What are you doing here? Get hungry again, did you?"

"I come to fill that woodbox for you like I promised."

"Well, that's sweet of you, but I see no reason why it can't wait until morning."

Randy said, "I'll see to it now, if it's all the same to you. Pa says I give you my word, so I need to get 'er done."

Rule set his book down and stretched lazily. "How would you like a hand? It won't take long with both of us working at it."

Randy shook his head. "That's right generous, but I doubt Pa would cotton to the idea. It was me who said I'd do the job, so I reckon it's for me to do, alone."

Mrs. Hardt and Rule smiled at each other. Then she nodded. "All right, Randall. Stop in after you're finished, and I'll cut you a nice big piece of pie. How's that sound?"

"That would be swell, ma'am," Randy said. His supper was still waiting for him at home, but he didn't see any reason to confuse her with details.

"See you later, Mr. Callum," Rule said, and picked up the book again as Randy took his leave. Those words kept ringing in his ears and perked him up enough to catch a second wind. Nobody else had ever called him mister before, and he liked the sound of it.

Actually, it wasn't all that big a job, anyway. Mrs. Hardt always had a couple cords of firewood cut and split out back of the house. It was only a matter of hauling in the logs and dumping them in the woodbox. In only twenty minutes or so, the box was full to the brim, and Randy could almost taste that pie already. There were two pies sitting out on the kitchen table, one peach and one apple; it was a serious question which one he'd choose when the time came. He was half praying she'd see how hungry he was and favor him with one of each.

Randy splashed some water on his face and dried off with his sleeve, then moseyed back out toward the sitting room to collect his reward. Only this time, when he got out in the hallway, Mrs. Hardt was standing by the front door, talking softly to someone he couldn't see. Something about the tone of their voices made Randy hang back. He stopped in the shadow of the stairway and stayed out of sight when Mrs. Hardt turned around with a worried look on her face. The man on the porch came in behind her and Randy saw it was Franklin Daniels, the owner of Bannon's only bank. He didn't follow her when Mrs. Hardt went back in the sitting room, but stayed by the front door, twisting his fine beaver hat this way and that between his fingers.

He didn't seem to notice Randy there, and the boy was careful not to move and catch his attention. Daniels was a stuffed-shirt dandy Randy had never cared for. He was always strutting around in fancy Eastern clothes, with a way of staring down his nose at all the kids like they were no-account and criminal, just by way of being young.

Voices from the sitting room reached the hallway, plain as day; Randy cocked his head to listen, though there wasn't any need.

"Yes? What is it, Mrs. Hardt?" Rule's voice said.

"There's a gentleman here to see you. I know how you appreciate your privacy, but he's most insistent."

"What does he want?"

"I don't know, but he claims it is a matter of the gravest urgency." Mrs. Hardt didn't care for Franklin Daniels much either—anyone could tell that from the sound of her voice—but she didn't say anything against him, and Daniels himself hardly seemed to notice. Randy saw Daniels smile when she said that part about it being urgent and all, so he could tell she was using Daniels's exact words, and he thought they were pretty smart ones, too.

"All right, Mrs. Hardt. Show him in, please."

Daniels pulled himself up straight and sucked in his gut the fancy clothes were supposed to hide, but didn't. A gold watch chain hung at his vest, and he patted the pocketed watch often, as if to make sure it hadn't been stolen. Randy wondered why he didn't just march straight in and introduce himself. But that wasn't Daniels's way; he stood there stiff and formal until Mrs. Hardt came back to announce him properly.

"This is your visitor, sir," she said, leading him into the sitting room. "Mr. Franklin Daniels, from the Bannon bank."

Rule stood and offered his hand. "Ulysses Rule."

Daniels shook hands like Rule had offered him a dead fish. "No need to introduce yourself. I daresay the whole town knows who you are by this time." He was talking too loud, in a way that showed he was nervous. That seemed funny to Randy, that Rule could make the stuffy banker as jittery as most folks were when talking to *him*.

Daniels took in the sight of Rule's book and pipe on the table beside the rocking chair. "You seem to have made yourself quite comfortable here. Shall we talk here, or would you care to retire to someplace more private?"

"This will do," Rule said. "At least until I have some idea what you want."

"Of course. Mrs. Hardt, may I ask you to leave us now?"

"Could I bring you some coffee or anything, either of you?"

"Never touch the filthy stuff," Daniels said. "You, Rule?"

"No, thank you, Mrs. Hardt," Rule replied. "Perhaps later."

"Then I'll leave you gentlemen to your business." Mrs. Hardt came out then, and saw Randy right off. She put a finger to her lips to make him keep quiet, but then saw there was no need. She pointed toward the kitchen, but Randy shook his head. She shrugged and they both stood there, listening in without a moment's shame over it.

They heard Rule's rocking chair start in motion again, and a match strike as he lit his pipe. A chair groaned and squealed when Daniels eased his bulk into it. Mrs. Hardt and the boy grinned at each other.

"Please put that pipe down," Daniels said. "Must you blow smoke like a chimney while we converse?"

"Yes," Rule said. "Now, what is it you want?"

Daniels sighed and sniffled a little, theatrically. "Very well. I suppose you are not aware of who I am."

"You're the bank manager, I gather."

"I do not manage the bank, Mr. Rule. I own it. In fact, I possess nearly all the land and business holdings here in Bannon that are worth owning. In a sense, one could say that the entire town belongs to me."

"I was told all this territory belongs to the mining company."

"Mr. Taggart owns the rights to most of the surrounding properties, that is correct. Paper rights, Mr. Rule. Those holdings will not be officially transferred until such time as the mining company profits have paid back all the costs of initial development. I cannot, of course, disclose the exact figure, but I can say it is a considerable sum. We expect Mr. Taggart's operation to pay back a handsome dividend eventually, but until the mining company's bank draft is fully repaid, all that you find here is part of my domain."

"I see," Rule said. "Just what is your point?"

"You don't seem very impressed," Daniels said. "I imagine to you Bannon does not seem like a very important or valuable acquisition."

"I'm only wondering what this has to do with me."

"I merely wanted you to appreciate my authority. We have no mayor or city government to speak of here, but none is necessary. Whatever happens in Bannon happens because it has been personally considered and approved by me."

"You're the boss here. I follow that. Go on."

Randy heard the rattle of Daniels's gold chain, and he mimicked the banker's stuffy way of pulling out and studying his watch. Mrs. Hardt giggled.

"My time is important to me as well," Daniels said. "I appreciate and sympathize with your impatience. I will get to the point. It has come to my attention that you intend to hold a public hanging in my town."

"That's so."

"Then you must understand that such an event cannot possibly occur until it has been properly considered and approved by the local authority."

"You," Rule said.

"Exactly. I know that you are a stranger here and therefore did not know the proper procedure for such matters. That is why I have taken it upon myself, in this instance, to seek you out and talk through the necessary plans and details."

"Just what are these necessary plans and details you want to talk over?"

"Why, the whole event, of course," Daniels said. "It would be extremely imprudent to rush into any hasty action until we have considered the general welfare of the town at large."

"The question has already been decided."

The banker shook his head. "Forgive me, but I can't accept that. You are clearly not a businessman. Do you have any idea what hanging McAllister can mean to Bannon? The way such a barbaric act can stain the reputation of our town? No, sir, you certainly have not. You simply must reconsider."

"In other words, you want me to call off the execution?"

"Most probably . . . Well, yes."

Rule took a deep breath. "You want me to let a criminal go free who was responsible for the deaths of innocent men. Is that about the size of it?"

"Well, I would not put it in those terms, exactly."

"What terms would you put it in?" Rule's voice was flat and cold. "Exactly?"

"You state it somewhat crudely, but basically yes, I am asking you to drop the matter. I have spoken to the sheriff, and it is clear the case against McAllister is a shaky one at best; certainly there is some question about the legality of charges for crimes which occurred over ten years ago. We are worldly men, you and I, Mr. Rule. Surely we can reach a gentleman's agreement. No doubt you have incurred considerable expenses in the course of your duty, and it is only fair to see you properly compensated. I can promise a generous incentive in return for your cooperation."

"Just out of curiosity," Rule said, "how much incentive are we talking about?"

"I am prepared to offer you five hundred dollars cash money if you will ride out tomorrow and forget this whole unfortunate incident ever occurred."

Randy heard Mrs. Hardt gasp. They looked at each other, and her face was about as gloomy as the boy felt. Together, as if they both had the same thought, they edged closer to the door for a look inside the room.

"I have a simple answer for you," Rule said. "No."

Daniels grumbled, "Very, well. A thousand. That is a very considerable sum, probably more than you've ever seen at one time. It would be very wise indeed if you merely—"

"Save your breath, banker. That's all I need to hear."

"I see. Then we have a deal?"

"Of a sort. You leave now and I won't toss you out on your fat behind. Now, is that *gentleman's agreement* quite clear?"

The banker bolted to his feet, towering over Rule with his fists clenched. "Nobody speaks to me that way."

Rule stood up slowly until he met the banker's eyes directly. "Our talk is over, Mr. Daniels. You're leaving now, and I have one suggestion for you: Stay out of my sight. I never want to lay eyes on you again."

The banker flinched as if he'd been slapped across the face. "You are a very foolish man, Mr. Rule. I think you will be sorry you ever came to Bannon."

"You know the way. Follow your own slimy trail out of here." Rule sat back down and calmly touched another match to his pipe.

Like a man boxing shadows, Daniels swung at the rising smoke. His fist cut through the cloud, barely disturbing it. Disgusted, he shook a finger at Rule, his hand trembling.

"You will regret this, Rule," he sputtered. "So help me, you will wish you had never seen my face."

Rule smiled thinly. "That occurred to me right off."

With a grunt of rage, the banker spun on his heel and stormed out, right past Mrs. Hardt and Randy as if they weren't even there. The front door crashed shut behind him and rattled on its hinges.

Rule settled back in his chair, rocked back and forth gently. The smoke was coming out of his pipe like steam from a train.

Then he glanced up, saw Mrs. Hardt and Randy peering in the doorway. "Oh, Mrs. Hardt. I apologize for the commotion. The banker and I had a difference of opinion. You heard?"

"It was impossible not to overhear."

"I suppose it was."

She walked in, clung to the back of the chair Daniels had vacated, and stood there hesitantly. "Forgive me, Mr. Rule. I know it is none of my business, but I feel you must be warned. Mr. Daniels is a harsh man. He could make a great deal of trouble for you if you antagonize him."

"That barrel of tailored lard?"

She nodded somberly. "Don't underestimate him. He is a powerful man. No one can do business in this town without his consent. The mule trains that pass through here are funded totally by Taggart and by Daniels's bank. Nothing, not a scrap of food or a bolt of cloth, comes into Bannon unless it is transported by them. The trains are the lifeblood of this town. Without them we could not survive."

"I see," Rule said. "If you cross him he could literally starve you out."

"There is more than one way to reach the mining camp. He has threatened before to route the trains to avoid Bannon. If that happened, all that we have worked to achieve here would be for nothing. We wouldn't last one winter."

Rule nodded grimly. "I appreciate your predicament. Rest assured, Mrs. Hardt, I will do nothing further to antagonize your local tyrant. My business will be concluded by the end of the week. I should be able to avoid Daniels for that spell."

"I don't ask for my sake," she said. "I have told you this only because I don't wish to see you make trouble for yourself."

"Thanks, but your concern is unwarranted. I have trouble enough without looking for more. I want only to see my job completed and then move on. Fat bankers I can leave well enough alone."

Mrs. Hardt smiled softly. "I just thought you should know." She retreated a couple of steps, then added, "May I bring that coffee to you now?"

"I'd like that. Thank you."

She moved off to the kitchen. Rule set his pipe aside and picked up the copy of Dickens again. But the book lay in his lap, unopened. Randy wanted to say something to him, but didn't have a clue what, so kept his mouth shut. He didn't seem in a talking mood, anyway.

Mrs. Hardt returned with a tray carrying a pot of coffee and a wedge of pie for Randy as well. Rule drank in a distracted manner, the whole time staring out the window. For the rest of the evening he sat there, barely moving but for the gentle motion of the rocker. As though in a spell, he gazed through the glass at the distant trail snaking up into the hills. Night was falling and the shadows of the mountains gathered in the valleys, then crept across the hills, nearly within touch of the town.

But the darkness, when it finally did come, seemed to close in from all sides.

CHAPTER 7

RULE found Murtry kicked back on his chair, in the same pose as earlier, as though he never moved a muscle except when other people were around. His head turned at the sound of Rule's footsteps, and his eyes focused slowly, so Rule knew he'd been sleeping.

"He's still here, if that's what you come to check on," Murtry said. "Bet you want to talk to the prisoner."

"I do, but not yet. Let him stew a while. He'll be more talkative once you hear from the authorities."

"Well, I guess so—if we get the word to go ahead and hang him. Then he's liable to sing like a bird."

Rule went to the stove and helped himself to a cup of coffee. It looked black and bitter as though left over from the day before. Considering what he knew of Murtry's ways, it probably was. Rule sipped the brew cautiously and settled down on a chair across from the sheriff.

"A funny thing happened yesterday," Rule said.

"Yeah? Tell me about it. I could use a laugh."

"Someone stopped by the boardinghouse to see me last night. A gentleman named Franklin Daniels."

"That was no gentleman—that's a banker. What did he want? I know—bet he tried to make a deal for the gold in McAllister's teeth."

Rule shook his head. "He tried to pressure me into calling off the hanging."

"That so?" Murtry frowned thoughtfully and rubbed his shiny head to a fine gloss. "Must be McAllister owes the bank money. I can't see why Daniels would give a spit about him unless he was afraid that somehow it would cost him."

Rule took one more sip of coffee, grimaced, and set the cup down. "I couldn't figure why he was so interested, either. But he definitely was. He tried to buy me off. Offered me a fat bribe to leave town."

"Daniels was willing to *part* with money? That is strange. You really got me worried now." For a long moment, Murtry sat back, sawing at his teeth with a toothpick, then he glanced back at Rule and raised his eyebrows. "Did you take it?"

"No. I said a few things he didn't like and sent him packing."

Murtry sighed. "Wish he'd offered it to me. Why do things like that only happen to people with more morals than good sense?"

"Your turn may come yet."

"Hope so. I'll be straight with you—they want to pay me off, I'll be out of here so fast it will make your head spin."

"Right. Just so you leave McAllister to me," Rule said.

Murtry groaned softly as he stretched out his arms, a motion he repeated often, and which was his only known form of exercise. "You want McAllister, you can have him," he said. "That man's been a pure vexation to me from the moment we brung him in. 'Murt, where's my meal? Murt, bring me some water. Murt, how about bringing me something to read?' You'd think he was staying in some fancy hotel, and I was his personal servant."

"Well, you won't have to deal with him much longer," Rule said. "When do you expect to hear from the marshals?"

"Should know something in a day or two. What are you doing to keep yourself busy in the meanwhile?"

"I'm going to start preparations. First thing, I need a carpenter. You know a good man you can recommend?"

"A carpenter?"

"For the gallows."

"You gonna go ahead and build a gallows before we get word back from the Feds?"

"I'll be ready to proceed the day after we get confirmation. No point in any more holdups."

"Seems a waste to build anything special for this," Murtry said. "If it was me, I'd just string him up from a tree."

"I want it done right. A man's last moments on earth ought to be conducted with some dignity."

Murtry shrugged. "Suit yourself. It still seems a waste of good money to pay for something you use only once."

"A name," Rule said impatiently. "You know someone who can handle the job?"

"Well, the best carpenter in town I suppose would be Dan Callum."

"Callum? Randy Callum's father? Think he'd be interested?"

"Won't hurt to ask," Murtry said. "I think he's between jobs now, anyway. Probably at home if you want to look him up. Just head northwest till you see a place with flowers out front."

"Fine," Rule said. "I'll go have a word with him. See you later, Sheriff."

Murtry waved lazily. "I'll be here. Don't know which is the real prisoner, McAllister or me. I can't go nowhere while he's in custody. A plumb nuisance, he is."

Rule paused on the boardwalk outside to stoke up his pipe. As he did, he glanced back in the feed store, watched Murtry climb out of his chair, fetch Rule's coffee cup, and pour the contents back in the pot.

The Callum home was a small frame house, neatly white-washed and trimmed with bright blue paint around the windows and doors. A short snow fence of wood slats ringed the yard like a small fortress. Clinging to the fence was a growth of wildflowers, a few with buds still showing. Rule wondered how the flowers had survived so late in the season while all the surrounding land was parched and fading into the muted tones of autumn. It was a small outpost of color in an otherwise gray little town, and someone had tended it with great care.

Rule knocked and the front door swung open as though someone had been waiting on the other side. Randy smiled up at him. "Hi, lookin' for me?" he asked.

"Not this time," Rule said gently. "I'd like your father to do some carpentry work for me, if he's interested."

"He's in the kitchen—come on in."

Rule stepped inside and right away he caught a whiff of bread baking. He lifted his nose and sniffed appreciatively. Randy led him straight to the kitchen at the back of the house. Dan Callum was seated at a table in front of a large window which looked out over the hills beyond. Randy's mother was in flour up to her elbows, and several loaves of bread were sitting out to rise. They both looked up, surprised, when they saw who their son brought in with him.

"This is Mr. Rule," Randy said. "See, told you I knew him."

Dan Callum frowned uncertainly, then stood up and came over with his hand out. "Morning, sir. Sorry I didn't greet you at the door. We weren't expecting visitors."

Rule shook the hand offered him. "Sorry to drop in on you like this. I wanted to catch you before you go off to work somewhere."

"No problem finding me. Randy and I finished a job yesterday; now all I'm doing is figuring what to do next and hoping something will turn up. More hoping than figuring, actually."

His wife broke in gently, "Dan, offer the man a seat."

"Oh." Callum pulled out a chair at the table. "Rest yourself, Mr. Rule. Forgive my manners. Let me introduce my wife, Sarah."

"Can I offer you something to eat, Mr. Rule?" she asked. "It's no bother."

"Truth is, I had my breakfast already. But that bread smells too good to pass up."

Sarah smiled. She fetched a plate and knife from a cupboard, then carved four thick slices from a fresh-baked loaf and set the plate in front of Rule.

"Go ahead," Callum said, "don't be bashful. Sarah's bread is known all over town."

Rule slathered a slice with butter and dug in as if he were half-starved. "That's about the best I ever had anywhere," he said, and obviously meant it.

Sarah poured a cup of coffee and brought it over. "Shameless flattery," she said, then laughed. "But that's all right. I like it."

Callum sat back and folded his arms together across his chest. "So, what brings you here? Randy hasn't caused you any trouble, has he?"

"Not at all. Actually, I wanted to see if I could interest you in doing a job for me."

"Like I said, work's scarce lately. I'm interested. What do you need done?"

"A gallows."

Randy's parents exchanged an uneasy look. "So what I've heard is true," Callum said. "You intend to hang Tom McAllister?"

"That's so," Rule said. "In a few days, most likely. There isn't much time."

"I never built anything like that before. I'm not sure I know what one looks like."

"It's not much, just a platform with a trap door in the center, and a stout beam overhead, braced well enough to support the weight of—"

Sarah motioned sharply to her son with a toss of her head. "Randy, why don't you step out on the porch while your father and Mr. Rule discuss their business."

"Aw, Ma. They're not going to talk about nuthin' I don't know about already."

"No arguments, young man. Take your schoolbook with you and do some studying while you wait. Your lessons are going to start soon, you know."

Rule turned to the boy. "Your mother's right. You want to do good at your schooling, don't you?"

"Oh, school's okay. But I don't see why I have to study now, before it's even started."

"You know, I was in school for sixteen years," Rule said. "And I look back on it now as the best time of my life."

"Sixteen years?" Randy blurted. "Why so long? Did you have to take all your subjects twice?"

"Randy!" his mother said, chiding him.

Rule laughed. "I went to college," he explained. "To a beautiful old school in Scotland, almost halfway around the world."

"I didn't know you had to have so much learning to hang people."

Sarah hurried over and steered Randy away. "That's enough from you. Go now, no more stalling. And don't forget the book."

"Okay, I'm going." The boy glanced back at Rule. "*Sixteen years? Really?*"

"Afraid so," Rule said.

"Well, I guess it didn't hurt you none."

"Not too bad," Rule said.

Randy shuddered at the thought of all those years cooped up in a schoolhouse. Then he saw his mother's frown. He snatched up his book and darted from the room.

The adults got quiet, waiting till Randy was gone. He opened the front door, then closed it again good and loud, then tiptoed back till he could hear what they were saying. He knew it was a sneaky thing to do, but it seemed unfair, them talking behind his back that way.

He heard Rule say, "He's a good boy. You must be very proud of him."

Callum said, "Yes, we are. But some days he can try your patience. Other days, he's even worse. The wild notions that leap into a boy's head—it's a wonder where he ever comes up with it all. He really seems to have taken an interest in you, you know."

"Lots of folks have a morbid curiosity in what I do. Likely he'll get over it. So, you want the job?"

Sarah spoke up quickly, "I'm sorry, Mr. Rule. I don't think that's possible. Do you, Dan?"

"I guess not," Callum said, taking his cue from her. She had spelled out her feelings for him, plain enough. "Truth is, we could use the money. But we don't feel right about this hanging business, Sarah and me. Killing is against our beliefs, and I can't see my way to have any part in it."

"That's right," Sarah said. "Taking a human life . . . the whole idea is sickening. We can't get involved in something we believe is morally wrong."

"Fair enough," Rule said. "I'm sorry you feel that way, but I wouldn't want you to do anything against your principles."

Callum said softly, "Wish I could help. It goes against my grain to turn away a customer. Anything but this, I'd be only too happy to build whatever you want."

"I hope you aren't offended, Mr. Rule. We don't mean to imply any criticism of you. It's just that my husband and I hold our values very dear, and we believe that all violence and killing is abhorrent. We truly are sorry."

"Don't be," Rule said. "I respect your beliefs. The fact is, I feel much the same, myself."

Callum said, "Really?" He sounded doubtful.

"In fact, I do. I understand a hate for violence. Violence *is* repugnant. An evil, and I see no good that comes from it."

"Yet you're planning to hang a man. How can you say you are appalled by killing, when that is the very thing you are about to do?"

"I've seen too much violence, firsthand, to pretend it is anything but sickening. But there are men who cannot be reasoned with. Still, they must be stopped, a balance weighed."

"I'm sorry," Callum said, "but that sounds like a hollow

argument to me. There must be ways to change men for the better. Killing them doesn't solve anything."

"Neither does leniency. You can keep him behind bars all his life, and it will still never bring back the lives of his victims."

"Is Tom McAllister truly a murderer?" Sarah asked. "He seems a decent man. What's he supposed to have done?"

"I'm sorry, but I prefer not to talk about that just yet. The entire case might come to nothing. Of course I don't foresee that happening; still, it's best if I hold my tongue a few more days."

After that, they were silent for a long time, as if they knew they'd reached a point where they couldn't agree, and all decided to back off, from politeness.

"Is that true what you told Randy?" Callum asked after a few moments. "About all the schooling you had?"

Rule said, "I was going to be a doctor. I spent a couple years at the medical university in Edinburgh."

"What happened? I mean, your business now is a far cry from doctoring."

"The war happened," Rule said. "When the hostilities began, I left college to come back and serve."

"I guess the war changed things for a lot of people. You ever think of going back to finish?"

Rule shook his head.

"Seems a shame. There's always a need for a good doctor."

"The kind of medicine I saw practiced during the war convinced me otherwise. Butchery. Besides, by the time it all ended, I had other concerns."

"You mean, what you're doing now?" Sarah asked.

"In some ways, the war ended—in other ways, it's still going on."

Callum said, "You seem a decent man, Mr. Rule. I can't build what you need, but if you like, I could recommend another good man for the job."

"Thank you. I would appreciate that." He pushed his chair

back. "Well, I've taken up enough of your time. Thank you for the food, Mrs. Callum. It was memorable."

"It's no more than we'd do for any visitor," she replied. "Dan and I believe in treating all folks the same, even misguided souls engaged in the Devil's work."

"Sarah?" her husband said, a little angrily.

"I'm sorry, but that's how I feel. And I don't see any reason to mince words about it."

"No harm in plain talk," Rule said. "An honest word clears the air. Now, if you'll direct me to that carpenter, I'll be on my way. Good day, ma'am."

"I'll walk you out," Callum offered. "Do me good to get some air."

Their footsteps sounded on the wood floors, and Randy hotfooted it out the door, and plunked down on the edge of the porch. By the time they appeared behind him, he had his nose in a book and appeared to be studying for all he was worth. He pretended barely to notice they were there.

Callum walked down into the yard, but Rule paused on the step beside Randy and said, "Good book, huh? You learn a lot?" Slyly, he reached down and turned the book right side up in Randy's hands. In a whisper, he added, "From what you *heard*?"

Randy looked up, and Rule gave him a grin.

Then Callum cleared his throat, and Rule turned back to him. "Please don't be offended by what Sarah said. She's just not sure how to take a man like you. Sometimes she speaks her mind just to sound out an argument for herself. Especially when there's no one eager to take the other side."

"No need to apologize. I'm not running for any popularity contest. She can think poorly of me, if it suits her. I'll live."

Callum jammed his thumbs down in his belt and stared off at the mountains, up toward the direction of the Taggart mine. "Women don't always see all sides of a man," he said. "And maybe that's for the best."

"I suppose that's so," Rule said.

The mountains were snowcapped and gleaming in the sun, a vision of breathtaking beauty, but Callum's eyes were distant and a little sad. "I've worked with some rough sorts in my day," he said. "You know, I believe you're probably right, there are some men just can't be changed; there's evil in 'em, a core of pure meanness beyond control or redemption. But Sarah, she has more faith than me—she believes any man can be changed for the better. And I love her for that belief. I love her for her faith, and for a whole lot more—" He shook his head and smiled a little sheepish. "I guess I'm not making much sense."

Rule said quietly, "I don't think bad of a person just over a difference of opinion."

Callum nodded gratefully. "I guess that's all I'm asking." He explained then that the carpenter he had in mind, Ed Shaunessey, lived in a cabin outside of town, and pointed out the way for Rule to follow. "Ed's a suspicious ol' coot, though. Hard of hearing and wary of strangers. He's liable to take a shot at you before you can explain what you're after. If you like, I can go talk to him for you."

Rule nodded. "That's a kind offer. Go ahead and hire him. If you say he's the right man, that's good enough for me." He dug into a pocket, then handed over a fistful of money. "Pay him a retainer. That should cover it and his expenses."

Callum's eyes got big. "There must be fifty dollars here."

"Anything above the cost of supplies he can consider an advance," Rule said. "Keep some for yourself, as a fee for all your help."

"I can't do that. I haven't done anything to deserve it."

"Suit yourself."

"You sure you want to trust me this much? You really don't know me all that well."

"I know Randy," Rule said. "A fine boy says a lot about the man and woman who raise him. I don't think you'll cheat me."

"Thank you, sir," Callum said quietly. "You can count on me to treat you fair."

They shook hands again. Rule waved at Randy as they went through the gate together. "Tell your ma where I've gone," Callum said to the boy. "And don't wander off. You stick close to home and help your ma till I get back."

"Yes, Pa."

The two men went their separate ways, Callum heading off into the trees, Rule starting back into town. Randy watched until they were both out of sight, then stood up and tossed down the book. But he didn't get one step off the porch before a little cough froze him in midstride. He looked back over his shoulder, and there was his mother, standing in the doorway with her arms crossed and a frown on her face Randy didn't want to consider.

"You heard what your father told you, young man?"

"Yes'm."

"Come on then, there's wash to hang out. And while we're doing that, you can recite to me the lessons you read in that schoolbook."

Randy hung his head and turned back around. There were days he wished he was still a little kid, young and foolish enough to run away from home.

CHAPTER 8

RANDY'S father didn't come home till just before supper-time. The first thing he did when he finally showed up was tell Randy to find Rule and tell him that it was all fixed: Shaunessey would build the gallows, and promised to get right on it. By that time, Randy had tolerated about all the staying at home a boy could reasonably stand, so he was glad to do what his father asked.

He headed toward the boardinghouse, figuring Rule would be sitting down to his own supper about that time. But when he got there, Mrs. Hardt said he'd just left. Ben Hecht had dropped by with a message from Murtry, she explained, and Rule had taken off to see the sheriff. She didn't know what it was about, though.

Randy supposed he could have left his message with Mrs. Hardt, but it seemed more fitting to deliver it personally. Besides, he was curious what Murtry had wanted with Rule, and this gave him a perfect excuse to drop by and see for himself. So he thanked Mrs. Hardt and rushed downtown.

He got as far as the general store, where he spotted his friend Bill Kitson sitting out front with his boots up on the hitch rail, sipping a bottle of sarsaparilla. That wasn't something you saw every day, so naturally he had to stop and ask where Bill got money for the drink.

"My pa had a run at cards this afternoon," Bill said. "Drew a five and a six to an inside straight, and won hisself near two hundred dollars. Pa give me a whole dollar for myself, and said to go celebrate."

"What's your pa doin' in town?" Randy asked. "Why isn't he at work up in the mine?"

"Mine's having a slowdown. They wanted five or six miners to lay off for a week, and Pa volunteered. Said it gave him a chance to come into town and make some real money for a change."

"A slowdown? Why's that?"

Bill shrugged. "Search me. Pa says they's moving more rock than ever, but it ain't paying out at more than three hundred ounces to the ton."

That sounded worrisome. "The mine's not played out, is it?" Randy asked.

"Naw," Bill said. "Pa thinks they just strayed off the vein, and is stoppin' to think how best to refind it. Hell, they sent the other laid-off miners down to Catton City for a week, all on Mr. Taggart. He wouldn't throw away that kind of money if there was a chance of trouble with the mine, now would he?"

"No, I guess not. They really done that, huh?"

"Pa was supposed to go with them, too, but at the last minute he slipped away and come here instead. Said there's too many card pros in a place like Catton City, and he felt it in his bones this was where his luck would be." Bill grinned and shook his head. "Gotta hand it to my pa. He sure is the top dog when it comes to luck."

Randy didn't say anything to that. Bill's father had plenty of luck, all right, but most of it was bad. He'd gambled or drunk away every dollar he'd ever made, and probably more. Everybody knew the Kitson family was in debt to their eyeballs, and if it weren't for Bill's mother taking in sewing and laundry, there wouldn't be a roof over their heads or food on their table. The Kitsons were the poorest people in the whole town, but you'd never know it by Bill—he never had a care in the world and was proud of his father just as if he brought home a regular pay voucher, like everyone else.

That was partly why Randy admired Bill. Bill Kitson didn't have much to give anyone but friendship, but with that he was never stingy, so Randy liked him fiercely, and figured to keep on liking him, even if he did have a blind side when it came to his pa's virtues, or lack of same.

Bill took a big swig of his sarsaparilla, rocked back and patted the seat of the chair next to his own. "Sit with me a spell," he said, "and I'll buy you one of these, too. I still got some of Pa's money left. Besides, there's lots more where it come from."

Bill didn't get a chance to show off very often, so Randy hated to spoil it for him, but it just wasn't the right time. "Sorry, I can't do that. I got to go see Mr. Rule."

Bill made a sour face. "I wouldn't be too excited 'bout seeing a pantywaist like him," he said.

"What you mean by that?"

"Didn't you hear? That lily-livered hangman showed what he's made of—and it ain't much. Can't hardly call him much of a man at all."

"That's a lie!"

"What are you gettin' so riled about?"

"You take that back, Billy Kitson."

Bill sneered. "I won't, neither. That fancy pants showed his true colors today. The whole town saw him for what he is. Happened just a couple hours ago in the saloon. Two men, Greene and Younger, they called him out in front of everybody."

"What did they do that for?"

"Rule was asking a lot of questions about McAllister, and did anybody know anything about some of his old friends from back in the war. Greene and Younger told him he was annoying everybody and to clear out. Said they didn't care to socialize with his sort, and he'd better run out of that saloon if he knew what was good for him."

"Those two goons was probably just sore because of the way Rule and Murtry put them in their place the other day when they arrested Mr. McAllister."

"The hangman didn't look so tough when he was by

himself. He let them say those things to his face, and didn't even raise his voice. Or his fists, neither."

Randy frowned. "If Rule didn't fight them, it's because he had a good reason."

"Yeah, he did," Bill said. " 'Cause he's yellow."

"He is not."

"Is so. He's got a yellow streak down his back a mile wide. What else you call it when a man won't stand up for himself?"

"Where'd you hear all this?" Randy asked.

"From Pa. He seen the whole thing. Plumb pitiful, he said. It half shamed him just to watch. He said it was the most disgraceful thing he'd ever seen."

"I should of known if it happened in a saloon your pa would be the one to see it."

Bill bristled like a cornered tomcat. "What do you mean by that?"

"Just what it sounds like," Randy said. "Your pa's a no-account, and a drunk besides. He's not fit to shine Mr. Rule's boots, much less criticize him."

"You got no call to badmouth my pa." Bill shot to his feet so fast he knocked over his drink, and didn't even seem to notice.

"Well, I didn't mean to say that," Randy said. "But it's done said now, and I can't take it back."

Bill waved his fist. "You will, or I'll knock yer block off. Don't think I can't do 'er, neither."

Things were getting out of hand. Randy didn't want to fight him. He waved his hand like the idea wasn't worth his time. "This is a stupid argument. I don't want nothing more to do with it."

Randy turned away, but Bill started down from the board-walk as if he were going to go after him. "That's it—run away, jest like your friend!" Bill yelled. "Sissyboy! You's two of a kind, you are. Run off, sissyboy, before you pee your pants or start to cry."

Randy kept on walking as if he didn't hear. His ears were

burning, and he felt his eyes starting to well up with tears of bitter frustration. Anger was churning sourly in his gut, and the feeling scared him. He wasn't afraid of Billy, he was scared of the anger he felt toward him then, and of what he might do if he didn't get away.

Randy could hear Bill laughing for a long time, and didn't dare turn around or so much as slow down. He felt numb all over. He walked the rest of the way, hardly aware of where he was. It wasn't till he stepped inside the feed store and saw Rule sitting there across from Murtry that he came to, and even then he didn't feel all put together straight.

Rule looked up and smiled as if he didn't have a care in the world. "Hello, Mr. Callum. Why the long face?"

"Is it true?" Randy asked, real low. "Tell me, is it true?"

"What are you talking about?"

Randy gulped and blurted it out. "In the saloon today. They say you tangled with Greene and Younger."

"Is that a fact?" Murtry said. "Don't seem to be making many friends here, do you?"

"That's never been a major concern of mine."

"Somehow, that don't surprise me much." Murtry grinned.

"Don't you know what folks are saying—they're calling you a coward. I heard that Greene and Younger said nasty things to you, called you all kinds of names . . . and you let 'em do it."

"I see," Rule said. "And that bothers you?"

"Yessir, it does. Don't it bother you?"

He sighed and put his pipe away in his pocket. "Let me explain something to you. I'm not in a very likable job. If I fought everyone who disagreed with me or what I do, I wouldn't have time to do anything else."

"But the whole town is calling you a coward."

"I been called worse," Rule said. "And you will, too, by the time you're grown up. Learning to put up with things you don't like is part of what it takes to become a man."

"Well, then I ain't so sure I want to grow up."

Murtry chuckled at that, but Rule silenced him with a look. "You don't mean that, Mr. Callum. Every real man gets people cross at him sometimes. The only man who doesn't have enemies is one who doesn't stand for anything. But you can't settle every argument with fists or guns. That's why we have laws, and courts and judges, to decide our disagreements fairly, without people getting hurt."

Randy shook his head. "Maybe that's how it is back East, where lawyers and judges is thicker than rabbits. But here in the West, a man's gotta stand up for himself. You can't back down and let folks push you around."

"All those two in the saloon did was badmouth me. Names do sting some, but there isn't one foul name in the world so bad that it's worth doing injury to another man over."

"I dunno," Randy said, thinking back to how he'd felt when Bill had been insulting him. "I'm not so sure 'bout that."

"Look, Mr. Callum. A fight between two grown men isn't like when you and your friends tussle. No one cries uncle, and it's not over soon as one gets the other on the ground. When men fight, someone gets hurt."

"Well, yeah. I know that."

"I'm not sure you do. A few bad words is a stupid thing to get yourself hurt over. I wasn't going to lose an eye or break some teeth just because some idiot called me a filthy name."

"Don't you have no pride? I'd rather lose a tooth than let someone hurt my pride."

Rule glanced over at Murtry and a little smile played at his lips, though he tried not to let it show. He reached out and patted the boy on the shoulder. "I'm glad you have pride, and don't ever let go of it," he said, quiet and solemn. "But you have to have brains as well. Pride without brains is just stubbornness."

"That's right," Murtry said, breaking in. "And even a dumb mule's got that much."

"I'm not sure what you're gettin' at," Randy said.

Rule sighed. "How would you have felt if I had fought with those two today . . . but *lost?* Would that have made you feel any better?"

"I don't really know," Randy said hesitantly.

"Don't you see—the only way I could win was not to fight."

"No, I don't, I don't get it at all."

"A fight would only have been giving them what they wanted—and I didn't intend to give them that pleasure."

Randy shook his head. "I don't know. . . . It seemed a whole lot simpler before."

"A simple answer isn't always best, just because it's easy. You have a good head on your shoulders. You just have to learn to use it."

"You're startin' to sound like my folks," Randy grumbled.

Murtry coughed then, and stretched out, groaning real loud as if to remind them he was there too. "You got a natural talent for making yourself important enemies, don't you? I guess Taggart must really have it in for you."

"You think he was behind it?" Rule asked.

"It's for sure Greene and Younger didn't take it on themselves. Those two couldn't build one thought together between them if they worked on it all day."

"What kind of man is Taggart? Tell me about him."

Murtry slurped his coffee. "Taggart? He is a different breed of feller, isn't he? Don't know what I can say about him 'cept that he's richer than God . . . and around here, he's got a lot more influence. He's the one what found the silver, and without the mine, there wouldn't be no town of Bannon at all."

"Yeah, I have heard that a few times," Rule said. "I think even Taggart himself told me the same thing."

"Well, he ain't in danger of winning no modesty contest, but what he said was true enough. Taggart's the brains behind it all. He started up the mining company, and he was the one who brought everybody together, decided what good people should stay, and what riffraff should stay out. Wasn't for him, we'd be just like all other mining towns, a city full of tents and shacks and people after nothing but a fast buck, here today and gone tomorrow. Instead, we built us something permanent here, something to hold on to."

Rule nodded and brought out his pipe again, smoked it quietly, lost in thought.

"Why so curious about him?" Murtry asked, after a minute. Rule sighed. "I'm just trying to put some things together. I don't see where McAllister fits in."

"McAllister was in the right place when Taggart struck the vein. He done all the initial assay work, and knew a good thing when he saw it, so he stayed. Probably all there was to it."

"He did what? McAllister an assayer?"

"That's right. He was at Northcamp from the beginning. That's where the mine is located. Way back in the hills. Bad country, nothing but rocks and snow, high up so it's winter year-round. A grimy hellhole, but there's silver there, so I guess it's worth a little misery."

"I wondered where the mine everyone talks about is. I haven't seen anything that looks like a shaft around here."

"That was the smarts of Taggart's plan. He figured to keep the mine and the town separate, instead of growing on top of each other like it happens most times. The miners stay up to Northcamp and work—hell, there's nuthin' else to do there. And we folks here handle the business side, haul supplies up to the mine and ship the silver down to market. This way, we get us a town free of whores and gamblers and con artists and such which foul every other silver town in the land."

"Sounds reasonable enough, I guess." Rule shook his head and knocked ash from his pipe into the bucket Murtry used for a spittoon. Then he stiffened as a shadow darkened the doorway. Rule's hand slithered inside his cloak.

Murtry glanced up. "No need to pull that Greener. Just more company is all. You want more answers about Taggart, now's your chance to hear from the man himself."

CHAPTER 9

MURTRY looked over at Randy and gave a toss of his head. "We got business now, boy. You go on now and leave us to it."

Randy nodded and Rule walked with him to the door. "Boy, things has sure happened since you come to town," Randy said. "Who knew so much was going on right here under my nose?"

"You better run along now. And this time no listening outside the door, all right?"

Randy lowered his eyes and nodded shortly. "Okay. Hey, I almost forgot what I come here for. I was s'posed to tell you: Pa fixed it with Shaunessey. He agreed to build the gallows for you, and he's starting work first thing in the morning."

Rule nodded. "Fine, thank your father again for me. Go on, now."

The boy turned away and walked slowly to the door. Taggart scowled down at him, then stepped aside. Randy stared up at him for a long moment.

"What are you looking at, boy?" Taggart growled.

Randy burst out the door without answering and ran off down the street. His footsteps faded away quickly.

Taggart shook his head, then nodded to Murtry and Rule, and with exaggerated courtesy said, "Gentlemen. Glad you both could be here. Now, maybe we can straighten a few things out. This unfortunate misunderstanding has gone on long enough."

"What misunderstanding is that?" Murtry asked.

"Don't play games with me. You got my partner locked up in this dump, and I mean to get him out."

"I don't know how you reckon to do that. Unless you think you know something we don't."

"Mac isn't a criminal—you know that much, don't you?"

"He ain't done any criminal act in this town, at least none I know of," Murtry admitted. "But what he done before he came here is something else. And Rule's paper says—"

The veins in Taggart's neck stood out tautly. "I don't care what any damned paper says. You have no right to keep him locked up. Where is he, anyway? What have you done with him?"

Murtry jerked his thumb toward the rear door. "He's shut up in a grain bin out back."

"Well, get him out here. We're going to talk this thing out, and he's got a right to defend himself."

"This ain't no court," Murtry said. "Talking won't change anything."

"What are you afraid of, Sheriff? What's wrong with hearing the man out? I mean to see him, and I don't aim to stand around in some filthy feed locker to do it."

Murtry looked at Rule, who just shrugged and said, "I'd be interested in what he has to say, myself."

"All right, all right," Murtry grumbled. He got up slowly, but before going to fetch McAllister, he drew curtains across the windows and carefully locked the front door. Crossing the room to the rear door, he took a ring of keys hanging from a nail, selected one, and slipped it into the lock. The door swung open with a loud groan. In the corridor beyond, the dust was even thicker than in the store, and the light spilling out from a single lantern was a muddy brown.

While the sheriff was thumping around in the back, Taggart pulled up a chair for himself, struck a match, and fired a fat black cigar. He tossed the match carelessly into the corner. Then he rubbed at some dust on his shiny boots, and glanced up at Rule. "You are a mystery to me, mister. I don't see what you stand to gain from all the trouble you've stirred up in my town. What's your stake in all this, anyway?"

"My interest is justice," Rule said. "I might ask you a few questions of my own toward that end."

"What would you like to know, Mr. Rule?" Taggart asked smoothly, waving his cigar. "I have nothing to hide."

Rule smiled. "That would be a nice change. People I run into often have a great deal to hide."

"Then you obviously run with the wrong sort of people. This time you have made a terrible mistake. I don't know what grievance you have against Tom, but I can tell you for a fact it's misguided. I've known Tom McAllister many years, and I swear that he is one of the finest and most law-abiding men in the territory."

"That doesn't say much for the territory, then."

Taggart smiled and stripped the ash from the end of his cigar with his little finger. "You won't get a rise out of me so easily, not this time. I admit that when we met, I may have acted a trifle unfriendly, but that's because it was all such a shock."

"Since you're in a generous mood, maybe you could help me. I'm looking for a man McAllister once was connected with, name of Evan Forrest. Could be he's mentioned him, sometime or another."

"And why do you want to find this man?"

"I intend to hang him."

Taggart scratched his chin thoughtfully. "You some kind of bounty hunter?"

Rule shook his head. "I don't take money for what I do."

"Really?" Taggart seemed truly interested. "How do you make a living?"

"How do you make everyone in this town do what you tell them to do?"

Taggart smiled. "I take your point. You have your business and I have mine."

"Just what is your business, Mr. Taggart?"

Taggart leaned back and spread his arms wide. "Look

around you, Mr. Rule. This town is my business. Everything you see, everyone you meet."

"I heard that already," Rule said.

At that point, Murtry came back, pushing McAllister in front of him. The prisoner's wrists were bound with handcuffs, and he shuffled along with short steps because of a fetter Murtry had tied between his ankles. Murtry pushed him down on a chair. "Stay there and behave yourself. Don't get any harebrained ideas about escapin'. I promise you wouldn't get very far."

"How am I supposed to run?" McAllister grunted. "You got me tied up tighter than a calf for branding."

"Don't give me no ideas," Murtry said. He dropped back onto his own chair with a weary sigh.

McAllister blinked while he got accustomed to the light. He looked at Taggart, and a glimmer of hope flickered in his eyes. "About time you came to get me out," he said. "What took you so long?"

"Business hasn't stopped just because you got yourself in a spot of trouble," Taggart said, nothing apologetic in his voice. "If anything, your absence has only made things more difficult. I came at the first opportunity which presented itself."

"Hell with business," McAllister spat. "You mean I been sweating in that damn hole, and all you been worried about is profits?"

"I haven't been idle, Tom. I have hired the best legal counsel in the territory, Mr. Deighton Kirby; he'll be here in a few days to personally handle your defense."

"Well, that's something, I guess," McAllister said, a little happier. "But a few days, you say? Can't you do something sooner?"

"I have tried a few other measures to get you released. It's not my fault those attempts proved unsuccessful."

"Glad you mentioned that," Murtry said. "Saves me the trouble of bringing it up, myself."

"What are you talking about, Sheriff?" Taggart asked.

Rule broke in, "He's referring to an attempt last night to bribe me into dropping the charges. Your friendly banker offered me a thousand dollars to leave town and forget the whole thing."

Taggart shook his head. "A bribe? Mr. Rule, I'm shocked."

"Yeah, I can see that," Murtry muttered. No one in the room believed Taggart, but he didn't seem to care.

Taggart stripped some more ash from the end of his cigar, let it drop onto the floor. "I wish someone would tell me what this whole thing is about. What did Tom do?"

"Nothing," McAllister said. "I didn't do nothing."

"Forgive me. What is he accused of doing?"

Murtry asked Rule, "What do you think? There's probably no harm in telling him, is there?"

Rule motioned for him to go ahead. He didn't seem to mind letting Murtry do the talking. He sat back and stuffed more tobacco into his pipe while Murtry told a short version of what McAllister had done during the war, how all those soldiers had died because of him and the smugglers he ran with.

"Very interesting," Taggart said, once Murtry wound up his story. "Very interesting, indeed." He looked at Rule. "Do you mean to say you've been tracking those six men all this time since the war ended?"

Rule said, "McAllister and Forrest are the last two and I intend to hang them both."

"You can't go around killing people," McAllister exploded, "like it was just another day of work."

Rule scowled at him. "And the men you killed at White-ridge? What kind of business did you call that?"

"It wasn't my damned war," McAllister raged. "I had a right to stay alive. We were just boys. We didn't know what the fighting was about. The generals didn't care about us, they moved us here and there like toy soldiers. We were nothing to them. When one of us died, they could always find another. They marched us into battle like herding cattle to the slaughterhouse. And for what?"

"I was there, too," Rule said. "Don't forget that. We were all scared and confused. Some of us broke down. Some ran for home and hid out the rest of the war. We all did things we're ashamed of. But only your lot sank so low as to profit by your countrymen's dying."

"We just did for ourselves what the generals were doing. What gave them the right to decide if I lived or died? My life was worth something, dammit!"

Rule said softly, "It could have been. But now your life is over. It's only a matter of days."

The prisoner glared back at him. "Think again, Rule. I'm not going to swing by your hand, or any other. It's not going to happen."

"Believe what you like."

"You don't scare me. By God, I'll make you pay for doing to me like this. I swear it."

Rule said, "Threats won't help you now. Calm yourself; here, have a smoke." He stepped up and held out his tobacco pouch.

McAllister's eyes widened. "What, is it poisoned?"

Rule laughed. "That's hardly necessary, considering. No? Well, suit yourself."

"Gimme a chance," McAllister said quickly, raising his manacled hands.

Rule held the pouch while McAllister dug out a fat pinch of tobacco. Murtry handed him a piece of newspaper. McAllister tore off a section of the paper and rolled himself a cigarette, then leaned over the match Rule struck for him.

He inhaled greedily, the end of the cigarette glowing red, then he was seized by a fit of loud, barking coughs. "Damn," McAllister wheezed, his voice thin and reedy. "You think that stuff's strong enough?"

"You're in an odd position to be particular," Rule said. "Give it back if it bothers you so much."

"You know, it does kinda grow on me after a while. Okay, what's the deal, Rule? Why are you being nice to me?"

"You figure I want something, heh?"

McAllister nodded and took another drag. "Yeah. So what is it?"

"Tell me where I can find Evan Forrest."

"Hell, you knew him as well as I did."

"You know what I'm after. Where'd he go after the war?"

"You gonna track him down and hang him too?"

Rule nodded stiffly.

"What do I get if I do tell you?"

"Nothing."

"How about a deal? I tell you where to find him, and you let me go. That's fair."

"No. No deals."

"Hell, I was never really one of them, anyway. It wasn't my idea to bargain with the Rebs. I went along because I had to. They would have slit my throat if I'd crossed them."

Rule shook his head and said quietly, "No deals, McAllister. You were tried and convicted by a court of military justice. I can't change your sentence, even if I wanted to. You help me just because it's right, a way to ease your conscience."

"My conscience don't need easing," McAllister said. "Aren't you listening? I told you I wasn't no traitor. It was just them, the others. They were the ones."

"Then you should be interested in seeing them all come to justice, like I am."

McAllister snarled and threw the stub of his cigarette down on the floor at Rule's feet. "What good will that do me if I'm dead? No way. I gotta get something in return."

Rule ground out the smoldering cigarette beneath his heel. "I don't bargain with other men's lives. That was your crime. I won't be party to the same mistake."

"Then I got nothing to say."

Murtry stood up and laid a hand on McAllister's shoulder.

"This ain't getting us nowhere," he said. "I think we all said what we have to say. Let's go, Tom."

"This has all been most enlightening," Taggart said. "I hope you gentlemen all agree that Tom's indiscretion in no way reflects badly on the company."

McAllister shrugged off Murtry's hand and glared up at his partner. "What! You mean to say that's all you care about—the damned company?"

"Of course not, Tom. Take it easy. It's just that, you know we are involved in some sensitive negotiations right now. This is not the time for—"

"You two-faced turncoat! I'm your partner, I got as much interest in the company as you or anybody. But this is my *life* we're talking about. What's that syndicate money mean compared to that?"

"That's enough!" Taggart snapped. "Shut up, Tom."

"What's that about a syndicate?" Murtry asked. "I ain't heard anything about that."

Taggart sighed. "The company is currently negotiating with an Eastern syndicate for capital which will permit us to expand and improve the operation. But outside investors can be very finicky—that's why I am so concerned that there be no hint of scandal or impropriety connected with the company at this time."

"Improve and expand, huh?" Murtry said. "Sounds real good. Could be just what we need to turn this town into something big. News like that could get folks real excited."

Taggart frowned and looked at the sheriff and Rule in turn. "I must ask you both to keep this information very confidential. There are lots of safer investments than mining operations for syndicates to sink their money into—it may well come to nothing. Promise me, Sheriff, that you won't breathe a word of this to anyone."

Murtry nodded. "I guess it wouldn't be right to get people's hopes up, if it ain't a sure thing."

"And you, Mr. Rule?" Taggart said, turning to the hangman.

"It doesn't concern me," Rule said. "I'll be moving on, once my business here is over. It doesn't matter to me if you sell the whole town, lock, stock, and barrel."

"Thank you, gentlemen." Taggart stood up. "I'll be back to see you again, Tom, once your attorney arrives. Keep your chin up. This will be ironed out before long, I promise you."

McAllister watched Taggart slip out the door, then Murtry headed him back to his cell. "You're just full of surprises, ain't you?" Murtry said to him.

The prisoner stopped and stared back over his shoulder out the open door Taggart had just left through. "How long you think it'll take for those marshals to get word back to you?" he asked.

"Hard to say. You'll know when we do."

McAllister cut his eyes over to Rule. "You really been after me all these years?" he asked incredulously.

Rule nodded. "All these years," he said softly. "I've been waiting a long time, but the waiting's almost over, just a few more days. The time will be gone before you know it."

"Sure, for you," McAllister grumbled. "But me, I got nothing else to do but sit and think about what's going to happen when we finally hear."

Rule nodded. "That's exactly why I don't mind waiting."

CHAPTER 10

THE morning meal was long over, and Mrs. Hardt's boarders were gone off on their own business. Rule found Mrs. Hardt in the sitting room, in her rocking chair, this time with a Bible open on her lap, and she was nodding over it as if asleep. He started to tiptoe past her, but the dry flooring creaked beneath his boots and her head came up. "Oh, Mr. Rule. Going out, are you?"

"Yes. Sorry, I didn't mean to disturb you."

"Don't be silly. Was there something you wanted?"

"Actually, yes," Rule said. "I heard there is a church somewhere outside of town. I was hoping to ride out there, have a talk with the reverend, but I'm not sure where to find it."

"You need directions? Certainly, it's about two miles down the southbound road. Shouldn't be too hard to find—I can't say for sure. I've never been out there, myself. Always meant to, but somehow I've just never found the time."

"You're welcome to come along, if you like."

She pursed her lips. "Well, I can imagine what folks would say, me stepping out alongside . . . that is—"

"With the hangman?" Rule finished for her.

"Well, yes." She looked up at him. "I hope you're not offended."

"Not at all. I appreciate honesty. Folks often mince words around me. It's nice to hear plain talk."

"I know the feeling. Once you reach a certain age people treat you as a child or a simpleton. Or a delicate heirloom they put in the corner and leave alone, afraid that it might break. I didn't live this long by being fragile, Mr. Rule, and I don't want to spend the rest of my years in anyone's corner. That's why I started this boardinghouse. Families can be almost too caring; in an odd way, strangers can be easier to deal with, less judgmental."

"I guess I never thought about it that way."

"I won't keep you. Have a pleasant ride, Mr. Rule. We won't have many fine days before winter. The cold weather comes around so fast here, and it seems to stay forever."

"Thank you, ma'am. Enjoy your reading."

She laughed. "Just between you and me, I'm a trifle super-stitious about Bible reading. I made a promise to the Lord a long time ago that I would learn His words to heart if he would just grant me the time to study them. So far He's held up His end of the bargain, but I'm afraid He might start complaining about the pace I'm proceeding to fulfill mine."

She picked up the book and adjusted the round spectacles on her nose. Rule left quietly.

Bannon's one and only church was well separated from the town proper, a short distance off the south roadway in a stand of tall timber. The sun was high by the time Rule left the wagon-rutted trail and moved into the trees. The pines were taking on a bluish gray cast, and here and there an aspen showed through with its autumn coat of pure gold. The brush was thick and tangled, so the going wasn't easy, and the path was hardly discernible.

The church itself was hardly more distinguishable. In fact, it was little more than a one-room box, with a spire nailed atop the roof like a last-minute afterthought. The yard was overgrown with weeds, and even the path to the door was choked with brush to a man's knees.

Rule tied off his horse, then waded through the under-growth and peered in the open door. Inside, it was dark and cool. Four short pews stood on each side of the aisle, and a number of oddly matched chairs were piled up at the back. The altar was a simple wooden podium that had been fashioned from a crate turned on its side. Behind the altar was a large hanging cross made of two shaved timber beams. The only other decoration was a small framed picture of Jesus, the face barely visible beneath its coat of dust.

The building was obviously deserted. Rule frowned and stepped back outside. He glanced around and detected a trail of trampled weeds leading around the back. Following it behind the church, he made his way to a small cabin set far back in a stand of trees, hidden from the road. He walked up and raised his fist to knock on the door when he heard a sound in the woods like the snap of a dry twig. Quick as a rattler, Rule darted into the shadow of the eave, and threw himself flat against the cabin wall. He withdrew the shotgun from beneath his cloak.

Rule peered into the woods, spotted a motion in the brush about ten yards off. One branch of a spruce tree was fluttering in a strange way. Then he heard the grumble of a muttered curse.

Rule trained the twin bores of his shotgun at the motion and stepped out. He shouted, "All right. Show yourself."

The movement in the trees halted suddenly. "Who's there?" a voice timidly called back.

Rule moved closer, waving the shotgun. "Move out here in the open," he ordered.

"All right, don't shoot. I'm coming out." A moment later, a small white-haired man appeared, his hands high over his head.

"Mister," the man said nervously, "you've made a sorry mistake if you think I have anything worth stealing."

Rule said, "I'm no thief. What do you want here?"

"I was going to ask you the same thing."

"That's not an answer."

"I live here. This is my church. I'm Pastor D'Argent."

Rule stared suspiciously at the pastor's rough clothing: a long plaid shirt worn as a jacket, denim trousers, and a shapeless, floppy hat. "You don't look like any minister I've ever seen before."

The pastor sighed. "I only have one decent robe. I hardly think it would be wise to wear it out fishing, do you?"

"Fishing?" Rule said numbly. He lowered the shotgun.

The pastor dropped his hands and pointed back in the brush. "I was just slipping away to a trout stream when you shouted and gave me the fright of my life."

"You fish barehanded, do you?" Rule asked, still suspicious.

"I caught my hook on a tree, and was trying to yank it free. It's true—come and see for yourself."

Rule tagged along as he backtracked a few steps into the trees. Then he pointed to a long wooden pole on the ground. "See? The cursed thing snagged when I was walking by, and it's caught like it will never come loose." He demonstrated by waving the pole. The branches of the snagged tree limb shuddered in response.

Rule laughed and put his shotgun away under his cloak. He studied the snarled line twisted among the tree branches and laughed again. "That used to happen to me when I was a boy."

"It still happens to me all the time," D'Argent said, and sighed. "I lose more flies this way."

Rule grabbed the line and gave it a tug. "I don't think this one's going to come loose," he said.

"Oh, I'll just cut it off." The pastor patted his pockets. "I have a knife here somewhere."

Rule slipped a hand into his boot top and pulled out his own dagger. The pastor's eyes got big, but he didn't say anything. Rule sliced through the line and handed the long part back to the churchman.

"Thank you kindly. Maybe I can do you a good turn someday."

"You might, at that. That is, if you really are the minister."

"I am. Phillip D'Argent, cleric and sometime catcher of trees, at your service."

"Ulysses Rule."

"I've heard that name somewhere. Now where . . . Of course." The pastor studied Rule with a grave expression. "You're the hangman, come to stretch the neck of that poor sinner Tom McAllister. It's a sad line of work you've chosen, my son."

"I came to ask you to take part. In the hanging, that is. It would be fitting if you would be there alongside McAllister and me, maybe offer a few words of comfort and guidance."

"Did McAllister ask for me?"

"No. But when the time comes, he might be glad for the chance at absolution. It's my experience that few men face eternity without a sudden hankering for conversion."

D'Argent nodded. "Just so. Even lifelong doubters like to hedge their bets, so to speak, when their final moment draws near. Of course I'll be there."

"I'd like you to offer a prayer. Something suitable and God-fearing, just a few well-chosen words."

"I shall be pleased to address the crowd," D'Argent said. "I daresay you can expect a larger attendance than I've ever enjoyed in my humble church."

"Short and to the point, all right, Reverend? Just a prayer, maybe, not a whole sermon."

D'Argent frowned. "Well, if that's what you think best."

"Have you ever attended a hanging, Reverend? I've seen a few. Believe me, the crowd will be in no mind to hear out a sermon. Many will be drunk, all of them on edge, knowing they're going to see a man die, and wondering how they'll take it. Worrying about his own squeamishness doesn't bring out the patience in a man."

"I take your point, Mr. Rule. I promise to keep my usual eloquence appropriately brief and restrained."

"Thanks, Reverend. Daybreak in the clearing west of town. I'll see you again, when I know the exact day." He glanced up at the snarled lure in the tree again and chuckled. "Till then, enjoy your fishing."

D'Argent picked up his pole and waved it in a practice cast. "Would you like to join me? I know a great spot where the trout practically jump out at your feet."

Rule hesitated. "It does sound tempting," he said.

"I have plenty of line. And a bunch of extra hooks." D'Argent glared at the tangled tree limb. "You can guess why. Any sizable stick will do for a pole. C'mon, I'd appreciate the company."

"It's a kind offer, Reverend. I can't remember the last time I sat down by a stream with nothing more to worry over than placing a straight cast."

"Good, it's settled then."

"Guess it is," Rule said. "Lead on, Reverend. I've never been one to follow in the path of the righteous, but I guess it's never too late to start."

D'Argent smiled. "Mr. Rule, I couldn't have put it better, myself."

CHAPTER 11

THE pastor told Rule to leave the horse, and assured him there was no danger of it being stolen, not enough people came by there to worry about. Rule laughed and said it was no problem, his horse had an evil temper around strangers; anyone brave enough or dumb enough was welcome to try.

Then the pastor led him into the woods. They walked about a half hour, the land getting steep and rocky. It was rough going. D'Argent was older than Rule, but the minister set a pace that left him dragging. He was tempted to beg for a breather when D'Argent pointed to a cleft between two sheer walls of stone. "Just through here," he said. "A few minutes more, and we can get down to the real business."

Rule followed him into the cleft. It was nothing for the slightly built minister, but a tight squeeze for Rule, the opening barely wider than his shoulders. Once through, they found themselves in a valley. The stone walls fell off into beds of gravel at the bottom, where a narrow stream of clear, cold water ran fast, breaking into small white explosions where it struck the larger rocks.

"Beautiful, isn't it?" D'Argent said.

Rule nodded. "It is." He looked around with a surprised expression on his face. "And quiet."

"The wind can barely reach down here," D'Argent said. "The trees and the stone muffle everything else. The sound is rather like that in some of the fine old churches I've visited in Europe. Perhaps that's why I like it here so much."

The pastor sat down on a large flat stone that hung out over the river. "I'm the sort of fisherman who doesn't much care whether he hooks anything or not."

D'Argent leisurely baited his hook with a fly he had been carrying in his shirt pocket. "I suppose I just like the excuse for a walk. It's important to get away now and then, and feel that one has somewhere to go."

Rule sat on the rock beside the pastor and accepted a length of string from D'Argent, then secured it to the first suitable stick he found near to hand. The pastor produced another colorful fly for him and tied it to the end of his string. Rule cast out into the water, then lay back, resting his head on the trunk of an old birch tree. He closed his eyes and let out a long sigh.

The pastor said, "Sometimes I come here and do nothing but sleep the whole day. It doesn't much matter, you see. I love it here. I think I feel closer to God in the forest than anyplace I've ever been. And I've visited some of the grandest cathedrals in Europe. But this place, this is where God lives."

"You could be right," Rule muttered drowsily. "I know I've seen damned few signs of Him anywhere else."

"That's a bitter thing to say. I sense a lot of anger in you, Mr. Rule. I gather life for you has not been kind."

"I'm not complaining."

D'Argent stepped up to the water's edge and cast his line far downstream. Then he looked back at Rule over his shoulder. "No, but are you happy?" he asked.

"I don't seek happiness, I don't even know how to define that. I'm proud of what I do, and the fact I do it well."

"What about family and friends?" D'Argent asked.

"My friends died during the war. Now I'm a hangman."

"I see. You mean hangmen don't have friends?" The pastor smiled at him to soften the words. "Try down there by that fallen tree. Trout often lie there in the shade during the heat of the day."

Rule tried another cast out where the pastor had indicated. Right away, he felt his line quiver. A nibble. A long shadow passed through the water a few feet from the line.

The pastor was still talking. "Do people treat you differently because of what you do? Make you feel like an outcast?"

Rule shrugged. "I'm used to it." He pulled out his pipe and began filling it from his leather pouch. "Let's talk about something else."

D'Argent pulled up his line, then cast out again smoothly. Rule saw something big and silvery flash just below the water's surface. Just as quickly, it was gone, no evidence in sight but a ripple spreading on the water.

D'Argent tied a different fly on the end of his line, then sent it sailing once more with an easy flip of his wrist.

Rule pulled in his own line, thinking to cast closer to where he'd seen the trout rise.

The pastor said to him, "You're not alone, you know. No one is truly an outcast. You don't have to feel that way."

"You trying to tell me I need religion?"

"I'm just making talk," D'Argent said in a lazy, idle way. "But since you brought it up . . . do you believe in God, Mr. Rule?"

"I don't know whether I do or not," Rule said. "I believe in justice. In seeing things put right, in the here and now."

"I hope my questions haven't offended you. I'm just curious about how other men view God, where they think He fits into their lives."

"I'm not offended," Rule muttered. "I'm just not used to talking about such things."

"I find it hard *not* to think about God when I come to this place," D'Argent said. He paused and looked around casually. "Here, among all this natural splendor, the glory of the trees and the river, the quiet. I feel close to God in this spot."

"I bet I'm not the first person you've brought here, am I?" Rule asked.

"No, actually you're not."

Rule smiled. He set his fishing pole down on the ground, lay back, and closed his eyes.

Right then, his pole jumped a good foot, skittering toward the water. "Grab it," D'Argent said. "You got him."

Rule clamped down on his pole, hefted it once, and shook his head. "Nope. Think I just lost my hook." He hauled in his line and sure enough, the trout had made off with D'Argent's fly. Rule shrugged and laid the pole back down.

Then, out of the blue, the pastor asked him, "What's your father like, Mr. Rule?"

"That's a hell of a thing to ask. Where did you come up with that?"

"You don't have to tell me."

"My father? What he's like mostly is dead." Rule opened one eye and peered at the preacher suspiciously. "You sure are one for odd questions."

"My curiosity is endless," D'Argent said, chuckling softly, "and I'm not bound by such trivialities as politeness."

"I've known you one hour, and I figured out that much for myself."

The pastor pressed him, "Well, what was your father like? Was he a good man?"

Rule sighed and settled back down, closing both eyes again. "He was. A quiet man. He liked to read; he could sit all day with a book and forget everything else. It was as if the world couldn't touch him. But of course it did."

"How do you mean?" D'Argent said.

"My father ran slaves on the underground railroad, helped them escape to the North. He thought the others he was involved with were in it for the same reasons he was. They weren't—his partners were charging the slaves twenty dollars a head. For freedom . . . When I hear politicians talk about the cost of liberty, that's what comes to my head: twenty dollars. When slavers came along and offered those men a better price, they sold out. My father tried to put a stop to it. The slavers came to his house one night, dragged him out, and beat him to death on a public street. Nobody raised a hand to stop them."

"I see," D'Argent said thoughtfully. A ripple flashed on the water far across the stream. He raised his head and ran a finger along his line, testing its pull. Then he glanced back at Rule. "Do you think your father would be proud of what you do?"

"I don't know. Maybe. I don't see the point of asking questions that can't be answered."

"Come, now. You must wonder about such things sometimes."

"I know who I am and what I stand for. That keeps things simple. The here and now is enough for me to deal with."

"Yes, living is tricky. Uncertain and risky, so easy to lose sight of the truth." D'Argent stared off across the water. "We wade through life as if fording a fast-moving stream, and without the solid footing of truth, we stumble and are swept away."

"I guess that's one way to look at it."

"That's why I come here, to remind myself of God's truth. It's too easy to lose sight of God while going about the business of living, the chore of getting through one day after another. But He is here, in plain view."

"You are ministering to me, aren't you? You are one sneaky preacher."

"I'm merely pointing out what is already visible. His image is all around us. The truth is here, for all to see."

D'Argent's pole suddenly fluttered up and down in his hand, and he looked up, felt the line with his free hand. "Hey, I think I have something."

Rule said, "Maybe you do."

CHAPTER 12

THE two men got along so well they talked the day away, and it was nearly dark when Rule finally got back to town. The sun was low over the mountains, and he stopped to look up at the clearing on the hill. Shaunessey had gotten a good start; the framework of the gallows could be seen, right in line with the setting sun. He dismounted and walked the rest of the way into town to let the animal cool off. The air was damp, as if it were going to rain again, and chimney smoke hung close to the ground, like a fog of soot and ash.

He strolled slowly past the mining company. Curtains were drawn across the windows facing the street, and inside Taggart's office a single dark figure was etched by the glow of lanterns. Then the figure backed away from the window, vanishing like a ghost. Rule walked on by, showing no concern.

Deciding to check in with the sheriff, Rule headed for the feed store. When he started past the saloon the doors swung open and Murtry stuck his head out. "Rule, in here," he said, and ducked back inside without any more explanation. A loud gust of laughter reached out through the open doors. A friendly, welcoming sound.

The saloon was no more than a large single room with plain board walls that had once been whitewashed, but now were soiled from tobacco smoke and soot from the winter coal stoves. Square rough-built tables were jammed together covering almost all the floor space. On the opposite wall the bar was chest high, topped with stretched burlap. Behind it, the owner, Clayton Fowler, drew beer from wooden kegs and tossed together concoctions from an assortment of colored bottles on three shelves.

Murtry had a table to himself next to the front windows. There was a big glass of beer in front of him, and he was eating a fat sandwich made of the leftovers from the free lunch. Rule walked straight over and pulled out a chair across from him.

"You didn't leave McAllister alone, did you?"

Murtry shook his head. "Ole Larson's watching over him, give me a chance to eat my supper. Don't worry, McAllister's snug as a bedbug. Nobody picks trouble with a blacksmith, specially not Ole Larson. He ain't known for a gentle disposition."

"You always take your meals here?"

"It suits me," Murtry said. "The food's not much, but it slides down good when the beer is cold."

Clayton Fowler walked out from behind the bar and headed their way. He was a large beefy man with a smile that never changed, one expression for all occasions.

"Barkeep's comin'. Don't mind his face," Murtry whispered. "Fowler is from Canada, and some folks claim a smile froze on his face one winter and never thawed. You ask me, he's just too stingy to give away anything for free, even a clue to what he's thinking."

Fowler came straight up to their table and said, "Evening, Mr. Hangman. I didn't think we'd see you in here again, after that trouble the other day."

"What trouble was that?" Rule said.

"You know . . . well, have it your way. What can I get for you?"

"What do you have?"

"We got home-brewed beer. Also watered-down whiskey, or any mixed drink you can think of, but none you'd care for."

"Make it a beer," Rule said.

"Wise choice." Fowler glanced over the sandwich Murtry

had prepared for himself, then shook his head and muttered to himself as he went back behind the bar.

Rule turned back to the sheriff. "So, what's up? You heard the news we've been waiting for?"

Murtry took a moment to wash down a big bite of sandwich, then wiped his lips with a sleeve. "Well, I heard something, all right, but I ain't sure it's exactly what you was hopin' for."

"There some problem?"

"Depends on how you look at it. The marshals sent us an answer. A rider came in this afternoon."

Rule said, "And—?"

But Murtry clamped his mouth shut, for right then Fowler came back and plunked two drinks down on the table. "There you go," he said. "Two dollars."

Rule frowned. "Kind of steep, wouldn't you say?"

"Yep. But no arguing is gonna change it. Still want it?"

Murtry leaned over and said, "He's not ribbin' you. That's what it costs. Every time the supply wagons are late, the price goes up."

"That's the price," Fowler said. "Either pay up or wait till tomorrow. Price might drop again, if you're lucky."

Rule set two silver dollars on the table, and Fowler scooped them up in the blink of an eye. He didn't move off right away, but lingered to watch Rule tip up his beer and take a long drink.

Rule finished his drink and saw the bartender was still watching him, waiting. "It's good," Rule said.

"See there. Worth two dollars, ain't it?"

"It's good," Rule said again.

The bartender laughed dryly. "Okay, I'll take what I can get."

Murtry groused, "At these prices, you got no right to compliments too. You mind, Clayton? We're tryin' to have a talk here."

"Sorry. Must be a special moment, havin' someone actually

listen to you." Fowler flashed that frozen smile across them once more, then went back to his place at the bar.

"You were saying?" Rule said.

Murtry sighed. "Yeah, right. A rider came in a little bit ago with a message. Some message, too. Wait till you hear it." Murtry took a piece of paper from his pocket and unrolled it. He squinted for a moment, frowned and pulled out his spectacles, then read, " 'Received your inquiry concerning the arrest and possible future execution of one individual by the name of Thomas Bentry McAllister. Our office has no record of any outstanding warrants against the aforenamed person, but as the alleged offense occurred during a state of war, and the trial was conducted by a military tribunal, the army has been duly notified, and a prompt response will be shortly forthcoming.' "

Murtry paused to catch his breath. "Whew," he said, "and some folks accuse *me* of being long-winded. He sure does sling a lot of words together to say how much he doesn't know."

"Is that all?" Rule asked, disappointed.

"No, no. I'm gettin' to the good part now." Murtry adjusted the spectacles on his nose and studied the paper again. " 'Due to the grave nature of the charges against Thomas McAllister, and because of many questions over the validity of a presidential commission allegedly granting one Ulysses Rule the authority to serve as official executioner, a formal hearing will be conducted at the earliest possible convenience, for the purpose of confirming the identity of the accused, and the validity of the charges against him. The Honorable Justice Warren Timmons of the federal district court has been dispatched to Bannon, and will oversee this hearing shortly after arrival. Since this matter is of the most serious consequences, it is strongly suggested that the suspect, Thomas Bentry McAllister, be taken into custody and incarcerated until such time as the hearing can commence.

Yours most sincerely, Jackson A. Purdy, Chief Federal Marshal, Montana Territory.' "

Murtry took off his specs and put them away in his pocket. "So, what do you make of that?"

Rule frowned. "More delays. They're wasting our time and sending that judge on a long, unnecessary trip."

"Well, now," Murtry said. "It doesn't seem to me all that unsensible, considering. The war was over a long time ago, and the charges against McAllister ain't fresh in anyone's mind."

"Except in mine."

"Ask me, they're right to be cautious. After all, if you're going to string a man up, it seems only reasonable to make sure he's the *right* man, and that the charges are still legal."

"I'm positive about both matters."

"Then you got nothing to worry about, do you? It strikes me that this judge coming might be more of a godsend than you realize. Especially for you."

"What do you mean?"

"This hearing will give the whole town a chance to hear the charges against McAllister, and if he's found guilty by a federal judge, there's no one can argue against it. Might make the whole thing go a whole lot easier than if it happened merely on the word of Ulysses Rule."

"I guess you could look at it that way," Rule admitted.

"Trust me. Once this judge arrives, the townspeople will take to you a whole lot more."

"It doesn't matter much to me what they think," Rule said. He paused thoughtfully, then motioned to the note in Murtry's hand. "You told McAllister about that yet?"

Murtry grinned and shook his head. "I saved that little chore for you. Thought you might get a kick out of it."

"You mind?"

"Not at all," Murtry said. "Take your time. It'll give me a chance to sit here and catch a little rest."

Rule thought if Murtry were any more rested he'd be in

danger of being mistaken for a stone, but he kept that thought to himself. He gulped down the last of his beer, then pushed back his chair and got to his feet.

Outside, night had fallen; overhead was a moon of polished gold, shining like the dreams of Coronado. It was so bright Mrs. Hardt could have brought her Bible outside to read. Rule stared up at the moon as if it were saying something only he could hear.

When he heard someone call his name, it took him a moment to realize the sound wasn't merely in his imagination.

CHAPTER 13

RANDY had been sitting on the tailgate of a wagon in front of the general store when he saw Rule come out of the saloon. He waved his arms wildly and yelled again. "Mr. Rule. Over here!" This time Rule saw him, waved back, took up the reins to his horse and strolled over.

As Rule started across the street, Randy's father came out of the store balancing two large sacks of flour on each shoulder. He dumped them in the back of the wagon, brushed off his hands, then glanced over at his son. "What's all the hollering about?"

"I saw Mr. Rule come out of the saloon. He's comin' over to talk with me."

"That so?" Callum said. He looked back over his shoulder at Rule, then hitched his thumbs in his belt and waited. Sarah took a receipt from the grocer, Mr. Lawrence, then stepped down from the sidewalk to Callum's side. She didn't look overly pleased to see Rule, but her husband's smile seemed genuine enough.

"Evening, Mr. Callum," Rule said as he walked up to them.

"Evening," Randy and his father both said, echoing each other. Callum grinned at his son.

Callum said to Rule, "Been over sampling Fowler's home brew, have you?"

"I needed to talk to the sheriff a minute."

"I see," Sarah said frostily. "And you naturally decided a saloon was the best place to do that?"

Rule spoke quietly. "That's where he happened to be."

"And that beer on your breath," she snapped. "I suppose that just happened as well?"

"I drink a beer now and then, sometimes two. But I'm no boozer."

"There are plenty of men in those places who are," she snapped. "And I don't care for people who socialize with them."

Rule smiled. "Well, with booze costing what it does in this town, I should think your average drunks would be priced out of business."

"Fowler really took you, did he?" Callum asked.

Rule shrugged and motioned toward the wagon. "Looks as though things for you are picking up," he said. The wagon bed was filled with sacks of flour, beans, coffee and sugar, and a dozen other foodstuffs, enough to last a family for weeks.

"It's not exactly all paid for. Mr. Lawrence advanced us credit when he heard I would be working for Taggart."

"Pa's goin' back into the mines," Randy said.

Rule looked at the carpenter. "I didn't realize you worked in the mines before, Mr. Callum."

"Oh, sure. Most of my working life I been fitting support beams and framework in one mine or another. I started here doing that when we first came, but Sarah frets about it so much I promised to make a go of things above ground if I could."

"I hate every minute he spends in those shafts," Sarah said. "It's not a natural way to make a living. And it's dangerous. I was so thankful when I thought he was out of them for good. He promised he'd never enter one of those shafts again."

"So why the change of heart?" Rule asked.

"No choice in the matter," Callum replied. "Nothing else in this town for me to do. It was fine for a while when all the construction was going on, but for now they've done built almost everything they can build. Times is hard, I gotta do what I can to keep my family fed."

"So you still set on staying around here a while longer?"

Sarah broke in again. "Where else could we go? Another mining town? Wherever it is, we've already been there. This is the fifth mining town we've lived in since Randy was born. Dan has dug for gold or silver in every part of the Rocky Mountains. Enough, I say. This town is different; it's somewhere we can make something permanent, and we mean to stay."

"Even if it means breaking my promise," Callum added, with a glance his wife's way. "We'll do whatever we have to do to stay here . . . even go back underground for a stretch."

"I'm sorry times are tough for you," Rule said. He squinted at Callum. "It must have been hard for you to turn down my offer of work."

"It was. Honestly, it was."

"Your principles cost you some, didn't they?"

Sarah stepped up and clung to her husband's arm. She raised her head proudly. "We get by, Mr. Rule. We're not rich and likely never will be, but we know what's important to us, and for our son. We can't give Randy everything he wants, but he'll have everything he needs, you can count on that."

"I believe you, ma'am," Rule said. "He's a fine boy, and I think, a very lucky one."

There wasn't much she could say to that. Sarah was in a mood to argue, but Rule wouldn't give her anything to complain about.

"We got enough food to feed the whole town," Randy said, pointing to the wagon. "Mr. Rule, how 'bout you come to supper and help us eat it?"

Rule said gently, "I think your folks have better plans for all that stuff."

"Naw. We'd love to have you to supper. Wouldn't we, Ma?"

He had her backed in a corner, and she knew it. "Well, Randy," she said. "I don't know. . . . "

"Why not?" Callum said. "Join us, Mr. Rule. First time

we've had a cause for celebrating in a spell. It won't seem but half a party without guests."

Rule shook his head gently. "Seems to me I've already asked enough favors of you. I don't want to put you to any trouble."

Sarah smiled at him almost sweetly. "No, do come, Mr. Rule. You can see we have plenty. Don't think you'd be putting us out. How about supper tomorrow?"

"All right, if you're sure," Rule said.

Callum said, "We'll look forward to seeing you. Come by the house around seven." He swept Randy under his arm and steered him to the wagon.

"Don't be late," Randy called to Rule. He jumped up into the back of the wagon. Sarah ignored her husband's offered hand, and climbed gracefully up on the seat; Callum bounded up beside her and started fussing with the wagon's sticky brake.

Randy looked back and waved again as he watched Rule grab up his horse's reins and trudge off in the opposite direction.

But Rule had taken only a few steps when a loud cry stopped him in his tracks. "Hold it right there, hangman!"

Three men tromped down the boardwalk toward him. Randy squinted to make out their faces. Taggart and his two pals, Greene and Younger. It appeared they'd been engaged in some serious drinking. Greene had an almost empty bottle in his hand; from the way the three men swaggered, and the look in their eyes, it was clear little of it had been wasted.

Greene looked at Rule, and a wide smile slipped across his unshaved face. "Look what we got here," he hooted. "Looks like somebody's chicken has escaped from its coop."

Younger laughed. "Oooh, it is not. It ain't nuthin' so respectful as that."

"Purely disgraceful," Greene muttered, "how some people let their varmints run loose on the streets. We ought to cage it back up, boys. Be doing the town a service."

Rule lowered his head and kept on, ignoring them. But Greene lurched out onto the street and blocked his way.

Randy tugged on his father's coattails. "Pa? Pa, wait." He pointed back at Rule and the three men closing in on him. Callum stopped the wagon and quietly handed the reins to Sarah.

"Dan, please . . . " she said, "it's not our concern."

"I'll just be a minute." Callum ran a hand through Randy's hair. "Stay put, boy." Then he swung down from the wagon.

"Dan, don't . . . " Sarah pleaded, but he didn't seem to hear. Callum started down the street, slowly rolling up his shirtsleeves.

Greene tipped back his head and took a long draft from the bottle. He wiped his lips with a sleeve and grinned at Rule. "Mr. Hangman, sir," he mumbled. "How fortunate we run into you. The boys and me, we been discussing an important question, but can't come up with no good answer. You must be a smart man, what with your fancy ways and smooth talk and all. . . . Maybe you'd lend us your opinion on the matter."

Rule said, "Why don't you go home and sleep it off?"

Greene laughed. "That's right, I'm drunk. Saw that right off, did you?" He turned and flashed a grin at his friends. "See, didn't I tell you he was a smart one?"

A few short strides brought Callum back to the general store, where he paused to draw a new sledgehammer from a display of miners' equipment. He slung it on his shoulder and then walked on.

Greene was still leering as he continued to pester Rule. "Now the question is, Mr. Hangman . . . There's a word we're trying to think of to describe the kinda man who ain't really a man at all. The kind of skittish fella who's kinda daintylike, and wouldn't raise his fists even if you spit in his face. You know the kind I'm talking about, Mr. Hangman?"

"Coward," Taggart offered softly.

"Yellerbelly," Younger hissed.

Greene shook his head. "No. Them's both good words, but not the one I'm trying to conjure up. But you, Rule—you're probably familiar enough with sissy-boys to recall the exact word I'm searching for. Heh?"

Rule scowled and flipped the reins lazily in his hand. "You want a fight, you go look somewhere else."

At that moment, Callum strode up and positioned himself at Rule's side. He took the sledge down from his shoulder and held it easily in one hand, swinging it idly. The three drunk men watched the hammerhead swing back and forth as though hypnotized by its motion.

"Sarah and I had a thought, Mr. Rule," Callum said. "There's no reason to wait till tomorrow. If it's agreeable, why not come to supper with us now?"

"Kind of you," Rule said. "But I may be a few minutes more. No problem, just a minor annoyance."

Taggart stepped up. "This is none of your business, Callum. Clear out of it!"

"That's true, it's not," the carpenter said. "I just decided to invite myself."

Taggart barked, "Step aside, Callum. You work for me now. Do as I say."

"I don't start till next week, if you recall."

"It's a sorry man who lets another do his fighting for him," Greene grumbled.

Callum shrugged. "That's how I feel about men who pick fights only when their opponent's outnumbered."

The drunken teamster scowled. "I don't need help against the likes of you."

A small crowd had gathered, men rushing out of the saloons and shops to watch the proceedings. A murmur went through them and one or two men egged Greene on: "That's telling him. Go ahead and show him what you mean. He ain't nothing but talk, anyway."

Greene flashed his supporters a grin, then squared off to Rule, his eyes glinting with malice. "Hear that? I ain't the only one sees you for what you are. The lowest form of vermin what ever strayed into this town. If you know what's good for you, you'll slink out the way you come in, before the boys and me prove it to you."

Rule continued toying with the reins of his horse in a bored manner. "That the best you can do? It's hard to get riled at a man who can't insult me any better than that."

"You smart-mouth," Younger growled. "We don't do our fightin' with words."

"Lucky for you," Rule said. "If brains were dynamite, you wouldn't have the charge to blow your nose." He sighed wearily and turned to Taggart as though the other two weren't worth his attention. "I don't know what you hope to accomplish with this. Let's end the foolishness and go our separate ways."

"My family's waiting, Mr. Rule," Callum said. He rested the hammer back on his shoulder. "I don't see any reason to hang around here, do you?"

Rule looked straight into Taggart's eyes and shook his head. "Nothing at all worth mentioning," he replied.

The hum that went through the crowd this time had a different tone. Angry, disapproving. It was becoming clear to them that nothing might come of it all, and they voiced their disappointment.

Greene's eyes darted around, then the gleam in them kindled into a blaze. His hand dropped to a sheath at his belt and he slid out a long-bladed knife. "That does it. I'm going to cut out that wise-ass tongue and silence it for good."

Suddenly he lunged, slashing at Rule's face. Rule side-stepped, then snapped the reins like a whip, raking them across Greene's eyes. Greene screamed and dropped the knife to clutch at the bloody gash on his brow. In the blink of an eye, Rule sprang behind him and slipped the reins around his neck. He yanked back hard, nearly pulling him off his feet, and Greene gasped as the leather straps tightened around his throat.

Younger dropped into a fighting crouch, but froze there when Callum gave him a demonstration with the sledgehammer. With a casual swing, he stove in the side of a watering trough, smashed clean through the hardwood sides without any apparent effort. He raised the hammer in front of Taggart and Younger and peered at them down the shaft as though it were a rifle barrel. The two men stared at the weapon respectfully and hardly even breathed.

Greene twisted and squirmed to break free, but the reins steadily tightened, cutting off his wind.

"You know," Rule said softly at his prisoner's ear, "hanging people teaches you a lot about the anatomy of a man's neck." He pressed his thumbs down on Greene's Adam's apple, and air wheezed out of him in a gravelly rattle. "All I have to do is press a little here." Greene jerked violently. "And you would choke to death. A slow, painful death, but a sure one. Nothing anyone could do to save you."

Callum looked over, his expression grave with concern. "You have his attention, Mr. Rule," he said. "So now what?"

"Worried I might hurt him?"

"You're *killing* him."

Rule shook his head. "Don't worry. I don't want his worthless soul on my conscience." He let the reins fall, then put his boot to Greene's backside and sent him sprawling. The teamster thudded to the ground at Taggart's feet. He rolled over once, still clawing at his throat, sucking in huge gulps of air.

"The fight seems to have gone out of them," Rule said. He smiled at Callum and added, "You wave a mean stick."

Taggart's face was livid. "I want you out of my town, Rule. Nobody crosses me. I want you out!"

"You'll have your wish. Just as soon as I've done what I came to do. I intend to hang Tom McAllister, and nothing is going to stop me from that, understand? Nothing."

Taggart scowled and opened his mouth to retort, but just then a lean, well-dressed man pushed through to the front of the crowd and caught his eye. Rule saw Taggart's attention shift, and looked to see who was responsible. He recognized the stranger from Mrs. Hardt's table, the one named Coleson.

"What's going on here, Taggart? Having some trouble?"

Taggart's spunk seemed to desert him. He dropped his shoulders and said quietly, "No, not at all. Just a little difference of opinion. It's nothing."

Rule said, "Finally, we agree." He smiled once more at Callum, then spun on his heel and led his horse off down the street. The crowd parted to give him wide clearance.

Greene struggled onto his knees, coughed, and spat in the dust. "That wasn't fair fighting," he cried hoarsely. "You seen it. He tricked me."

"Shut up, you fool," Taggart snarled. He started to turn away, but stopped when he caught sight of Callum still standing there with the hammer swinging in one hand. "You're through. You won't work for me, or for anyone in my town. You have a week to pack up and clear out."

Callum nodded solemnly. "If that's how you want it." He tossed the sledgehammer none too gently to Younger, who caught it awkwardly and stared at it as if afraid what it might do.

Callum trod back up the street. A few in the crowd stepped up as if to say something to him, but one look at his face, and they backed away without a word.

Randy hung over the side of the wagon and grinned proudly at his father as he came back to the wagon. "You really showed them, Pa," he said. "They were too scared to even fight you."

"Quiet, boy," Callum said. He climbed up in the wagon and took the reins from Sarah's hands, head down as if trying to avoid her eyes.

"I hope you're pleased with yourself," she said. "You call yourself a man of peace . . . but the first sign of trouble, you drop your principles and raise your fists."

"Sarah—"

"Whatever in the world came over you? What are we going to do now?"

"He was all alone." Callum sighed. "Did you want me to sit here and do nothing?"

"Fighting is not our way. At least, I always believed so."

Randy popped up from the wagon bed and wedged between them. "Pa didn't fight anyone," he said. "All he did was scare 'em a little."

"There, you see?" Sarah hissed. "The ways of the father, so becomes the way of the son."

Callum said softly, "Not now, Sarah. This town is spoiling to see a fight, but I don't think they need to witness anything as dirty as one of our spats. Let's go home."

He snapped the reins and the team strained against its harnesses. The wagon slowly rolled away. Sarah stared at her husband, and sniffled a little. "*Home?*" she said, and it sounded like the saddest word in all the world.

CHAPTER 14

RANDY couldn't wait to get out of the house. His parents bickered all through the night and by morning they still hadn't settled anything. It seemed they couldn't say two words to each other without getting into it again. They didn't fight the ugly way some married people fight—they were always civil and decent to each other—and though sometimes they raised their voices there was never a danger of their disagreement escalating into physical violence. But it was still nothing pleasant to overhear.

Finally, his mother took Randy aside and told him to leave and find something to do. He didn't need any more coaxing than that. He beat it out of the house as fast as his legs could carry him. And it took him no time at all to decide where to go.

When Randy entered the feed store Murtry rolled his eyes and said, "You again?"

"Seen Mr. Rule yet this morning?"

"I saw someone up on the hill earlier, headed for that contraption Shaunessey's building. Figured that was probably him, though it was too far off for my eyes to say for sure. He'll probably be in here before long, I know him."

Randy pulled up a chair and settled down to wait for Rule. Murtry didn't offer to let him stay, but he didn't say to get out, either. That was as much invitation as Randy figured he needed, certainly as much as he was likely to get.

"So, what do you think about all the goings-on yesterday?" Randy asked.

Murtry looked at him under droopy eyelids and said, "I

try not to think during workin' hours. Just gives me a head-ache."

That seemed all he was willing to say. He rocked back on his chair with his boots on the counter and dosed off and on for the next few minutes, every once in a while letting out a loud snore until his own racket seemed to wake him up, and he would look around a second, like a prairie dog checking for coyotes, then start the whole business over again.

Time passed slowly in that way. After a while Randy got squirmy and wondered if there wasn't someplace better to be. Just about the time Randy had waited all he could stand, Rule strode in and dropped onto a chair with a long sigh. Murtry opened his eyes a little wider, but still seemed unsure if he meant to keep them that way for long.

"Morning, Sheriff," Rule said. "You're looking well rested."

"No thanks to you," Murtry said. "You are definitely making an impression on folks here, aren't you? I never saw anyone except politicians or bank foreclosers who could turn people against them so fast."

"You saw what happened in the street yesterday, did you?"

"Could hardly miss it, could I? Watched it all from the saloon. Pretty sizable crowd watching, too. I don't recall I heard too many cheering you on, though."

"You didn't try very hard to stop it."

"Wasn't nothing to stop. Whole thing was over before I'd even finished my beer."

Rule glanced over at the boy. "If not for Randy's father, there might have been. Doesn't it seem odd that Taggart wants so bad to get rid of me? Why do you suppose he's doing that?"

"Don't know," Murtry muttered, shrugging.

"I know Taggart and I didn't exactly take to each other right off—"

"Yeah," Murtry said, "havin' a knife stuck to your throat can sour a fella some."

"Still, the way he's reacted doesn't make sense. You'd think a respectable businessman would be interested in learning the truth—in making sure his partner isn't the thieving murderer he's accused of being. But Taggart doesn't seem to care whether McAllister's guilty or not."

"Tom and Taggart are friends," Murtry said. "To some men that kind of loyalty is more important than the law."

"Still, his methods seem a little desperate. First he tried to bribe me, then to scare me out of town. Is that the way a legitimate businessman goes about getting what he wants?"

Murtry squinted at Rule. "What are you gettin' at?"

"Something more is going on here, something we don't know about. There has to be. And somehow or another, it involves that man Coleson. Did you see the way Taggart reacted when he showed up yesterday?"

"Yeah, I wondered some about the same thing, myself."

"Who is Coleson? What can you tell me about him?"

Murtry shrugged and stared out the doorway as he spoke. "Not much at all. He's only been in town a week or two longer than you. Arrived one day without a word to anyone, far as I can tell."

"He was staying at Mrs. Hardt's when I first came to town. But he moved out the day after I showed up. I wonder if Taggart had something to do with that."

Murtry shook his head. "If I knew anything I'd tell you. It's a mystery to me, same as you. I don't know anything about the man."

"I think we better start learning, and soon."

"All right, I can ask around," Murtry said. "But I wouldn't expect much. Near as I can tell, he hasn't had anything to do with anybody, except maybe Taggart."

"Just the same, see what you can find out. Meanwhile, I think I may do a little nosing around of my own."

"What you got in mind?"

Rule said, "I'm thinking about riding up to the mine. I'd like to see Taggart's operation for myself."

"A silver mine ain't got much to do with your business,

does it?" Murtry asked. "It's a long trip to make, unless you're sure there's a point to it. What you figure to learn there?"

Rule frowned. "I don't know. But it's sure not going to do any good sitting around here. Anyway, I'd like to learn more about what McAllister's been involved in lately. The judge is liable to hear testimony that McAllister and Taggart have done a lot of good for this town."

"So? That's true enough, you know."

"If it is, I'd like to know about it before the hearing starts," Rule said. "I'm the only one to make a case against McAllister—it would help if I knew beforehand what his supporters are likely to say, and how much of it's true."

Murtry yawned as if the mere idea wore him out. "You want to go gallyfantin' round the mountains, be my guest. I'll stay here and keep an eye on the prisoner."

"How's he doing?"

"Quiet enough, since he hasn't heard yet about the judge comin'. Thought you were going to break that news to him. Why ain't you done that yet?"

"I'll tell him now. In private, if you have no objection."

Murtry waved a hand in the direction of the back door. "Suit yourself. You know the way."

Rule got to his feet and slowly crossed to the back door. He took the keys down, fitted one in the lock and swung the door open. He glanced back once, then disappeared inside. His footsteps thumped on the loose planks inside the corridor, slowly growing fainter.

A minute later, Murtry suddenly pulled his boots down from the counter and stood up. He gave Randy a sharp warning look, then tiptoed across the room until he stood at the open doorway, where he cocked his head to listen.

Randy grinned and walked over to join him. Murtry frowned and tried to wave him back, but the boy ignored him. The sheriff couldn't raise much of a fuss without giving them both away, and he knew it.

"You keep your mouth shut, boy," Murtry whispered. "Not a sound, now. I mean it."

Randy nodded and moved up to hear better. It was dark in the corridor, then they saw a splash of light appear on the far wall as Rule found a lantern and lit it. The glow bobbed and weaved when he took the lantern down from its wall peg and carried it with him until he was in front of the grain bins.

Murtry and the boy edged down the corridor a little farther. They could hear a racket coming from the bins, a low rumble along with a soft whistle. McAllister was snoring.

Rule marched straight up and pounded his fist on the wall. "Wake up, McAllister."

The snoring ended and was followed by the squeak of a wooden frame, McAllister sitting up on his cot. His speech was slow and slurred by drowsiness. "Who's that? What do you want?"

"I want a word with you, McAllister. I have something to say you should find real interesting."

"You got nothing to say I want to hear. Where's the sheriff? I thought I told you to leave me alone."

On the far wall, a man's form took shape. Rule had set the lantern on the floor, and the light cast his shadow up on the wallboards, an image of him bigger than life.

McAllister's voice grunted, "How much longer you gonna keep me penned up in this dump?"

"That's what I came to tell you. You could be getting out soon. But only long enough to appear in court. The marshals are sending a federal judge to town to decide if they'll let me hang you or not."

"That supposed to scare me? It doesn't. You got no case against me, Rule. I'm not gonna hang for something that happened years ago. They got laws about how long you can hold something against a man."

"If it had been an ordinary crime you might be right. Treason isn't an ordinary crime."

"I never was a traitor. I fought for my country long and hard as you."

Rule snorted. "Who are you trying to impress? I was there. I know what you did, all too well."

McAllister coughed, and then there was a long silence. When he spoke again, his voice was softer, with a tone of bewilderment. "Why? Why are you doing this to me? What's in it for you?"

"I don't expect you to understand," Rule said. "It's something I have to do . . . because it was left for me. I'm the only one who *can* see to it—I'm the only one left. It's on behalf of the forty-three souls buried in Whiteridge."

"It wasn't personal, what we did," McAllister said. "It wasn't even my idea. I had to go along with the others. They would have killed me if I didn't."

"Save it for the judge. The hearing should be early next week. I just thought it was fair to warn you. Who knows? The war *was* a long time ago—maybe he'll go easy on you."

"I can't believe it's gone *this* far. Taggart's got to put an end to this. I'll go crazy if I stay in this place much longer."

"What makes you think Taggart is going to help you? What are you to him?"

"We're partners. People think he built this town all by himself, but it ain't so. We done it together. The two of us made something for ourselves here. I don't aim to leave it all to him because of some mistake years ago when I was just a dumb kid and too scared to know what's right."

"What part did you play in building this town?"

"Don't believe me, do you?" McAllister said. "It's true, though, just the same. Taggart was just another prospector with dreams of one big strike, like so many of 'em. I was an assayer over at Wilson Creek when he brought in the first samples. He was a joke in these parts then; everybody knew he was digging someplace high in the mountains, where no man in his right mind would go. But I took one look at those rocks and knew he'd dug his way straight into glory."

"I don't recall you ever talked about being an assayer during the war," Rule said.

"I wasn't one then. It's a skill I picked up along the way. You talk like the war was over yesterday, but it wasn't. I've had lots of jobs in the years since, but assaying was the one I liked the best, one I had a good head for."

"So you were the first to recognize that Taggart was going to be a rich man, and he's been grateful to you ever since. Is that how it was?"

"Hell, no," McAllister said. "I did a lot more than that. Taggart couldn't wait to show the world he'd found silver where no one else thought to look. But I convinced him to keep his mouth shut. To look ahead and see all that was possible if we kept our heads. Together, we took possession of all the land surrounding the mine, and even along the trail leading up to it. Only when we were in a position to control everything and everybody that passes through this territory—only then did we let word get out."

"I was wondering how you managed to raise the capital to build a whole town."

"It wasn't any trouble. Just *talk* of silver is enough to make people go off their heads. In no time at all we had investors *begging* us to take their money, to let 'em buy in."

"And I imagine you were only too happy to accept."

"No, it wasn't that way. You think you know me, Rule, but you don't. From the beginning, we had a plan. We didn't allow outside investors, only people who were willing to move here and help us make something of the place. People with skills or businesses that a town needs, people with families, a stake in the future. Most mining camps, somebody strikes ore and before you know it the place is swarming with speculators, gamblers, whores—anyone with a scheme to skin the others from their money. No place can survive that kind of thing, no matter how much silver there is to be brought out and spread around. In Leadville there was over one hundred saloons, not even counting the game houses and dance halls and fancy houses. We made sure that didn't happen here."

"I have a hard time picturing you as a community builder," Rule said. "Since when did you become so civic minded?"

"I grew up." McAllister sighed. "People change."

Rule said, "*Most* do. There were forty-three good men at Whiteridge who never got to grow older. How much did you make from that deal, McAllister? What was the going rate for dead men back then?"

"You won't let up, will you? Like I said, that wasn't my doing."

"How much? I've always been curious."

McAllister sighed again. "It wasn't like you think. Didn't any of us get rich from it. That money was long gone before I came here."

"A sad story. But somehow it's hard for me to generate any sympathy."

"What do you want from me, Rule? I can't change what happened now, even if I wanted to. And I do, you know. You think it hasn't haunted me, that I haven't thought about it every day of my life since then and wished it never happened? I knew those men, too, every one of them. Their faces haunt me in my dreams."

"I really wish I could believe that," Rule said. "There's a small measure of justice in that, if it's true."

"It is true. I swear it."

"It's not enough. Not even close."

"You're a hard man, Rule. Whatever it is you want from me, you can't have it. You can say or believe the worst of me, if that's a comfort to you. But I'm not as bad as you think. I'm just a man who made a mistake, a terrible mistake, and whether you believe me or not, I've paid for it."

"No," Rule said softly. "Not yet. But soon."

"Go away," McAllister groaned. "Go find somebody else to torment." He dragged himself across the tiny cell and back to his cot.

Rule grabbed the opening of McAllister's cell and shook the door so hard it seemed as if he would rip the hinges off.

"Look at me!" he yelled. "Look at me, McAllister. The next time we face each other, I'll be slipping a noose around your neck. And you know what? I'm going to enjoy it. No blindfold or hood for you—I want your eyes open, to see it all happen. To see my face. My face will be the last thing you see in this life."

"Leave me alone, Rule," came a muffled cry. "Damn you, just leave me alone."

The shadow of Rule slowly straightened and turned away. "Next time, McAllister. Next time. By God, it won't be long now."

Rule started back out the corridor, and Randy turned to sneak away before he caught them eavesdropping. But Murtry didn't budge. He didn't move even when Rule came back around the corridor with the lantern swinging gently in his hand. When he saw them he stopped short and his face darkened.

"You were supposed to leave us alone," Rule said gruffly. He didn't return the lantern to its wall peg, just set it on the floor.

Murtry slowly shook his head. "It's true, what he said. You are a hard man. I think it best you don't bother him anymore till this thing is settled."

"You taking his side now?"

"No sides to it."

Rule growled, "Nothing will save him from me. You may as well get that through your head. No judge or court in the world can save him from me now."

"That's no way to talk. You're forgettin' yourself, Rule. Just do as I say and leave him be. Tormentin' a prisoner ain't right, and I won't stand for it."

"Have it your way, then," Rule snapped. He brushed past him roughly and stomped out.

Murtry picked up the lantern and hung it back on the wall

peg where it belonged. "Don't know why it's so tough to leave a thing where you found it," he grumbled.

A moment later, McAllister's voice called out, "Sheriff, that you?"

"Yeah, what if it is?" Murtry yelled back.

"You keep that lunatic away from me, Murt. You hear me? You see to it that Rule stays the hell away from here."

"I will," Murtry said. "But not as no favor to you."

"You saw him—he's off his head."

"I'd be careful what accusations I was flinging around, if I was you. I haven't heard anyone call you the kindest soul around, neither." Murtry paused and shook his head. He looked at Randy, but he might have been talking more to himself. "There are times I think there ain't but one sane man in this town, and I'm it. Other times I wonder if I'm not being too generous about that."

CHAPTER 15

RANDY pulled a chair out from the table and motioned to it with a sweeping gesture. "Sit here, Mr. Rule. Next to me."

Rule took the offered seat and flashed a smile to the boy's parents. "You've gone to a lot of trouble," he said, looking at the spread Sarah had prepared. There were bowls of young potatoes, corn, beans, platters of ham and beef, and on a cutting board was a fresh-baked loaf of the bread Rule had liked so much the first time he was in the Callum home.

Callum patted his wife's shoulder and chuckled. "You should see what she can do when she cooks for someone she likes."

"Dan, that's no way to talk," Sarah protested. "Besides, this isn't so much." But she didn't try very hard to disguise her pleasure at their compliments.

For a minute they all sat as if wondering what to do next. Randy's stomach was growling, so he decided to get things started. "Will you say grace, Mr. Rule?" he asked.

"Now, Randy," Sarah said. "Don't put our guest on the spot. Maybe Mr. Rule isn't that familiar with prayers." She was watching Rule while she said it, and her smile was cool and brittle as quartz.

"I don't mind," Rule said, and bowed his head. "For the food we are about to receive, may we be truly grateful. And as we partake of the nourishment that gives us life, may we pause and remember to cherish that life, to always strive in our deeds and thoughts to prove worthy. Bless this house and the good people who reside in it, protect them from harm so that they might continue to honor our Lord and the word of truth which is our spiritual nourishment. All this we ask in the name of our Father. . . . Amen."

Randy raised his head and smiled at Rule. He grinned back, then reached for the potatoes. "Now?"

Randy nodded. "You bet."

"That was a lovely sentiment, Mr. Rule," Sarah said. "Are you a Christian believer?"

"Not so you'd notice. But there was a church in my past."

Callum pushed a platter of meat toward the hangman. "There you go. Wrap yourself around some of that."

Rule shook his head. "Thanks. What I have is plenty."

Sarah put down her fork and sighed. "Please, Mr. Rule. It's true Dan doesn't have work at the moment, but this is one family that has never gone hungry."

"You saw all the goods we got from the store," Callum added. "Don't think you're putting us out."

"Mr. Rule doesn't eat meat, Pa," Randy said quietly.

Rule smiled and said gently, "That's true. My eating habits are . . . a little peculiar."

"You really don't eat meat?" Callum asked.

"I would take some of that bread," Rule said. Sarah handed him the cutting board and sat back with a dazed look on her face, her own meal still untouched.

Rule carved himself two slices of bread, then glanced over at Randy. He had some beef on his fork and was studying it, wondering just what the objection to it could be.

Rule leaned over and spoke softly in his ear. "Go ahead. There's nothing wrong with it."

"Then why don't you eat any?"

"You really want to know?"

"Yeah . . . I think so."

Rule set his fork down and folded his hands together. "All right, then. Let me tell you a little story. You see, when I was your age we were very poor. We lived far out in the country and hardly ever went to town. The only food we had was what we could grow, and it was poor land so there wasn't much of that. And whenever supplies got low and there was almost nothing to eat, my mother would say, 'Well, there's always ol' Trooper.' "

"Trooper?" Randy asked.

"That was our horse. An old scrawny nag. Broken down and swaybacked, almost too old to pull a plow, but he was all we had."

"Yuck. Your ma wanted to eat your *horse?*"

"No, she didn't want to. But whenever things got tough and it looked like we might go hungry she would say that: 'Well, there's always ol' Trooper.' So I knew if we got really desperate at least we wouldn't starve, because we had that horse to fall back on."

"You didn't, did you?"

Rule met the boy's eyes and nodded grimly. "Yes, we did. There came one day when there wasn't a bit of food in our house. A mouse couldn't have found a crumb on the floor. I was so hungry I thought my ribs were going to push out through my skin. My father was off at his work and my mother was gone tending to a sick neighbor. All of us children were so hungry. All day long we waited for our parents to come home and bring us some food, but after a while I decided they weren't going to make it. If we didn't get something to eat soon we would perish on the spot."

Rule paused and looked around. Callum and Sarah were listening with the same rapt attention as their son. He took a deep breath and went on, "So . . . I was the oldest and knew it was up to me. I remembered what my mother always said, and I knew that the fateful time had finally arrived."

"You *ate* ol' Trooper?" Randy whispered.

Rule nodded. "It had to be done. I put down ol' Trooper, even though it almost broke my heart. I cut him into steaks and when my mother and father finally got home, we were sitting back with full bellies and licking the grease off our lips."

"I bet they were real proud of you," Randy said, "for saving your brothers and sisters from starving."

"Actually, my father gave me the worst licking of my life."

"Why'd he do that? I don't get it."

"When they came home, my mother sniffed the air and said, 'What's going on here? Where did you find that meat?' I told her straight out. 'Mother, I finally did it. I slaughtered ol' Trooper to save us from hunger.' You know what she said to me?"

"What?" all three Callums said at once.

"She said, 'I never meant for you to *eat* the horse. I meant when things got tough so we couldn't stand it any more, then one of us should climb on ol' Trooper and *ride* him into town to buy food."

Randy stared at Rule for a long moment, not understanding, then heard his folks break into laughter.

"It's a joke, huh? You were teasing me."

"Not a bit," Rule said.

"I dunno if I believe you."

"The fact is ol' Trooper was better eating than he ever was as a plowhorse. Even my father admitted that. He had three helpings, himself. Didn't stop him from whipping me, though."

After that, the mood at the table lightened and they ate and talked almost like old friends. After his second plateful, Rule pushed back from the table and got out his pipe. Callum got to his feet and tapped him on the shoulder. "Come on. Let's step outside to smoke."

Rule followed Callum out the rear door. Randy jumped up to trail along, but his mother stepped in his way. "Not so fast, young man. Aren't you forgetting something? Those dishes won't dry themselves."

"Aw, shoot."

He was trapped and knew from the look on his mother's face there was no point in arguing. So he took up the towel and began to dry dishes faster than he had ever dried them before. There was an open window near the kitchen table, and by staying close to it Randy could hear almost everything the two men said to each other, and even see them whenever he made an effort to peer out. In some ways, it was even better than sitting out there with them, for they said a few things they might not have if they'd known he was listening.

"Sorry for dragging you outside," Callum said to Rule once he stepped off the porch. "Sarah doesn't care for the smell of tobacco. I spend a lot of time out here of an evening."

The carpenter settled himself atop the woodpile and pulled a small black cigar from his shirt pocket. He offered the real seat to Rule. It was a handmade bench set on the porch, with a stump for a footrest. It was a wonderful spot where a man could sit in the shade, stretch out his legs, and watch the sun go down over the mountains.

Rule sat down and stoked up his pipe. "This is a nice home you've made for yourself," he said. "Must be something to have a place all your own, a place where you feel you belong."

"Where's home for you, Mr. Rule?"

"I move around so much I hardly even cast a shadow, much less put down roots."

Callum said, "You know, I've been wondering about that story you told at supper. About your family being so poor and all. But last time you were here, you said you had gone to Europe, studied to be a doctor. . . . "

Rule laughed. "The truth is I grew up in Pennsylvania, just around the corner from a bank and a grocery store. And my father owned both of them. I never went hungry a day in my life. At least, not until I joined the army."

Inside the kitchen, Randy felt his face flush red. So the ol' Trooper story had been nothing but a joke, after all.

"But you really don't eat meat, do you? Why not?"

Rule replied in a low voice, so Randy had to lean close to the window to hear him. "It goes back to a moment in the war. There was a mass grave, forty-three dead. They didn't try to bury all of them; instead they set them afire. The smell was so much like . . . Meat's just never appealed to me after that."

"I never got to the war," Callum said. "I was in the mines then, and the government needed minerals more than soldiers."

"You should consider yourself lucky."

Callum lit a match and puffed his cigar into life. Then he pushed the charred matchstick down until it was well buried in the soil. Like most men in the dry Montana Territory, he took few chances with fire. Though it had rained a good deal the past week, and the hazard at present was slight, he still went through the precautions from habit.

"I can't help feeling left out, somehow," Callum admitted. "It was the biggest event of my lifetime, probably of the whole century. And I'll never know what it was like."

"What it was, mostly," Rule said, "was long spells of boredom, broken by moments of pure misery. For three years we ate bad food, marched through mud, and slept in our own filth. We would pray for the enemy to start something, just to have something to take out our meanness on. Then a battle would commence and we would look back at those boring times as pure bliss."

"You saw lots of action, then?"

"More than enough to suit me."

"Were you ever tempted to run away?"

"Every day," Rule said. "The only men who didn't feel like that were too plain stupid to know better, or too sick and miserable to care anymore about living or dying."

"Hard to believe a man could reach that point," Callum said softly.

"A lot of us reached it and beyond. War's a strange business—you start out thinking it's the most important thing you'll ever do. But in no time at all you wind up thinking it hardly matters. Survival is all that counts. Wars are fought by men who don't care a whit about victory or defeat, who don't have anything on their minds but staying alive."

"Sure must be quite a test. I guess you find out what you're really made of. At least that's something."

Sarah was staring at Randy, so he moved away from the window and got back to work. He realized then he had been stacking all the dishes into one place. One cupboard was jammed full of platters, plates, and pans, a cupboard meant to hold only cups and saucers. He stole a glance at his mother and quickly set to straightening it all out before she noticed.

Rule's voice drifted in through the window. "Truth is only a comfort to those it favors. Some men are better off believing they're something they're not."

"You really believe that?" Callum asked. "It's something I've always wondered about—if I could have cut it or not—but I guess I'll never really know."

"I served alongside good men with all the courage in the world, and others who were afraid of their own shadows. It was no measure of how they stood up in a fight. Some cowards fought like demons, out of sheer terror. The truth is, you were better off next to a lucky man than a brave one. Good soldiers and bad died just as fast. Sometimes it seemed it was just one big crapgame, and luck was all we had going for us."

A shadow spilled across the kitchen table. Randy looked up to see his mother standing over him. "You've been wiping that same dish for two minutes," she said. "You're liable to wear a hole clean through it."

"Sorry, Ma," he said, and started to stick the dish up into the cupboard. That was a mistake. Her eyes followed the dish up to the cupboard, and when she saw the mess the shelves were in, she let out a little moan.

Sarah eased a plate out of Randy's hands and gave him a gentle shove in the back. "That's all right, I'll do the rest myself. You might as well go outside where you can hear better."

She didn't have to tell him twice. Randy ran out the doorway and jumped up on the woodpile next to his father. The two men exchanged serious looks and fell silent.

"Don't clam up now," Randy said. "You were talking about the war, weren't you? What'd I miss?"

"Through helping your mother already?" his father asked.

"Ma said I was done. She seemed scared I might dry the dishes into a hundred pieces."

Callum's arm settled around his son's shoulders in a casual manner. "What am I going to do with you?" he said with a sigh, but he didn't sound genuinely concerned.

The two men smoked and stared off at the mountains for a long time without saying anything. Randy fumed inside, angry they'd stopped talking about the war just because he'd showed up. "What side did you fight on, Mr. Rule?" he asked, to get things started again.

Callum tightened his grip and shook the boy gently. "That's not a diplomatic question to ask a man, son. The war is over now and people don't care to dredge up old arguments."

Randy wouldn't be put off that easily. "I bet you was in Union blue," he said to Rule.

"That's right. Missouri Cavalry."

"A horse soldier? Gosh, I bet you were a fearsome sight."

Rule chuckled. "Nobody seemed to notice, if that was so."

"A horse soldier is what I wanna be someday, too."

Rule shook his head and said sternly, "The day of the cavalry is gone. There's no point in charging a man on horseback, when he can cut you down with a rifle from two hundred yards, or tear you in half with a cannonload of canister. Horse soldiers got chewed up worse than most units. By the end of the war, they'd stopped using us for much besides mopping up, chasing down the enemy when they were retreating. Even then, we often came out on the short end of the stick. A horse is a big target, and a man riding high and pretty is just asking for it."

Randy frowned, thinking that over. "I dunno," he said. "Still think I'd rather ride than walk. Unless the army gives you real soft shoes."

Rule and Callum both laughed. "You have a lot to learn about army ways," Rule said. "God willing, you'll never have to. I hope this nation has seen enough war to last it for a long time."

"On that we agree," Callum said solemnly.

Rule stood up and tapped out the ashes from his pipe. He stared off at the horizon, where the moon was taking shape against the darkening sky. "Time I was going. But I'm grateful for a pleasant evening."

Callum got to his feet as well, carefully pinched off the end of his cigar, then put the stub in his pocket. "I was hoping to talk you into a game of chess. Or some whist, if you'd rather. No need to rush off."

"C'mon, Mr. Rule," Randy pleaded. "You hardly just got here."

"No, I should go back and get some sleep. Could be a long day tomorrow." Rule looked at Callum. "I'm planning to ride up and see the mine for myself. Take a look around. You have some ideas who I might talk to?"

"Concerning what, exactly?"

"Just about business in general. How production is going, how the men are treated, whatever comes to mind."

"Well, Ray Hodge and Sam Cobb are both good men. They're line bosses; they'd know how things are going, if anyone would. I'm not sure I understand just what it is you're after, Mr. Rule. Why the sudden interest in the mining business?"

"McAllister isn't the same man I knew ten years ago. I'm going to make some serious allegations against him in front of a judge. It strikes me it would help my case if I knew a little more about what he's been up to in all that time. And lately it seems to have been with that mine."

"Yeah, I did hear rumors about a judge coming. So we're

gonna have a real law-and-order trial, are we? That should shake up this town."

"I hoped it could all be handled quietly, but nothing has gone exactly as planned from the moment I arrived here."

"Know just what you mean," Callum said, and he sounded a little sad. "I really thought this time would be different. We spent everything we had to come here, but it seemed worth it, because we knew it was a place where we could make a home for ourselves. But I guess it wasn't meant to be. Now we have to start again from scratch, with even less than we come with."

"My fault," Rule said. "You wouldn't be in this mess if not for me. If there's anything I can do—"

Callum silenced him by raising a hand. "It was my decision, no one else's. Anyway, I never was too crazy about working for Taggart, you know. There's something about the man I just don't trust."

Rule looked up. "You feel that, too, do you?"

"I do. Have for a long time. Something in this town isn't quite square. Taggart's into some shady business, I think. It's only a hunch, nothing I can put a finger on, but I'm sure there's something suspicious going on."

Rule seemed to think hard for a minute, then he said, "Is there any chance I could talk you into going to the mine with me tomorrow? Help find out what that something might be?"

Callum shook his head. "Sorry. Like to help you, I really would. But I have to think of my family first. I'm going to ask around here for work tomorrow, see if anyone has the backbone to hire me against Taggart's wishes. If not, I guess we'll have to start packing up."

"I understand," Rule said. "I hated to ask. You've done so much for me already."

"I can take him, Pa," Randy said.

"Now, son. Mr. Rule might feel a little awkward about being led around by a young boy. He can find the mine on his own. After all, there's no big trick to following a few wagon ruts."

"The trail breaks off in two places," Randy said, "where it connects with the roads to Catton City and Windy Town. It would be easy to choose wrong there. Besides, I've been to Northcamp with you. The miners know me, and they wouldn't be so suspicious of Mr. Rule if I was with him."

"Well, that might be right," Callum said grudgingly. "You got this all figured out, don't you?"

Rule said, "It suits me. I'd be glad for his company. That is, if you have no objection."

"I don't know. His mother might not—"

"*She* can speak for herself," a voice said behind them. They turned to see Sarah looking out from the doorway. She smiled faintly at Randy. "And I say it's all right."

"Really, Ma?" Randy couldn't believe his ears. If she'd said that the sky was green and not blue he couldn't have been more surprised.

Sarah stepped down and ruffled his hair with her long, delicate fingers. "Yes. But only if you go straight off to bed now with no complaints."

"Thanks, Ma." Randy could feel his own face grinning so wide it almost hurt. "It's a long trip, Mr. Rule. We best get a start before sunrise."

"I'll be ready," Rule said. "See you then."

She gave the boy a little nudge toward the door. "You have to keep your end of the deal. Off to bed now."

Randy knew a bargain when he heard one. He gave her a kiss on the cheek—which surprised *her*; he hadn't done that in a long time without being asked to—and ran inside to go to bed as if it were the most exciting thing a boy could do.

Sarah went over and stood next to her husband, and he put his arm around her waist. "You think it's okay, don't you?" she asked him, as if still unsure, herself.

"Of course," Callum said. "Randy knows the way. He'll be fine. And Mr. Rule will see no harm comes to him."

Sarah turned slowly and looked at Rule. "You will watch over him, won't you?" she said. "Your word on it."

"You know I think the world of your son. I won't let anything happen to him."

"No, I know you do," Sarah said. "And I suspect you're a man of your word. What bothers me is how Randy feels about you. For some reason, he really looks up to you."

"And you don't like that."

Sarah met Rule's eyes and held them steadily. "No, I don't. Randy is growing up fast. We can't protect him from everything. It's time he learns that not everything in the world is exactly what it first seems to be."

"Meaning me?"

"Yes. I trust you, but not the same way Randy does. I trust you to be what you are. That's one quality I've seen in you— you're as straightforward as any man I ever met. But that doesn't make you right, or necessarily someone for a young boy to emulate. Randy won't ever believe that from me—he'll have to learn it for himself. People can't be counted on for anything but what's in their own self-interest. That's a hard lesson to accept, but he has to learn it someday. It might as well be now."

"What if your scheme backfires?" Rule asked. "You know, we could come back liking each other all the more."

She replied without hesitation, "Then I will be the one to change my mind about you. I have faith in my son's instincts, Mr. Rule."

"I feel like I'm on trial. All I wanted was a simple sightseeing trip."

Sarah laughed, but it was not a mirthful sound. "A trial? No, I don't think so. Trials are fair. I don't have to be."

CHAPTER 16

THE next morning Randy couldn't wait to get out of bed. It was still at least two hours before sunup when he decided he couldn't stand it anymore, got up, and tiptoed out of the house. The bay mare didn't seem that happy to be roused while it was still dark out, but he bribed her with a piece of his breakfast apple, saddled her, and rode slowly to the boardinghouse.

He expected a long wait, but when he got there Rule was already out on the porch, smoking his pipe and drinking cold coffee from the night before. His own horse was saddled and ready to go. "I don't ever sleep much," he explained while he swung up in the saddle. "Not since the war."

"Bad dreams, huh?"

"There's nothing in my dreams that doesn't haunt me as much during the day," he said. "But somehow the nights are worse."

If there was something on his mind, though, he kept it well hidden, and smiled the whole time they quietly rode out of town. Randy had a big grin on his face as well. It was a thrill for him to be up and at it while the stars were shining and the whole town was still asleep. There was something almost sly or secretive about it, which appealed to his sense of adventure.

They didn't talk much at first. It was cold and dark and they kept to themselves the way people do when staying warm is their main concern. But later, when the sun came out, they both opened up and by the time they reached the fork where the ruts veered off to Catton City, they had started to swap yarns.

Rule told him about strange and notorious hangings he'd heard about, like one in Jackson County, Missouri, where two men had been convicted of murdering a horse trader and sentenced to swing. The hanging party drank a lot of booze at breakfast, Rule said, then went to fetch the two murderers from the jail. There were only four prisoners in the jail at that time, and they had precise instructions which cell to find them in, so there was no worry about confusion.

The county hangman watched the ceremony from a river-bank, too far away to make out the prisoners' faces. After-wards, he went back to the jail and was recording the details when a voice called out to him from the cells. The hangman nearly perished on the spot from fright—it was the voice of a man who supposedly had just been hanged. The hangman went into the block and found the two murderers still in their cells. What's more, the other two prisoners in the jail were still there, as well. The night jailer said two drunks had been arrested but later released, and the arresting officer backed up his story. No one could figure out where the men they hanged could have come from. And they never did learn who they were. The county hangman lost his job, and the judge ruled that the whole business was botched so badly that eventually he let the murderers go free.

Then Rule said he'd heard of another case where a man was sentenced to hang for killing a woman in a fancy house. Three times the lawmen tried to hang this man, but some-thing always went wrong. First they stood him on the back of a wagon with the rope strung over the branch of a tree. But when they shoved him off the wagon, the tree limb broke. For their second try, they took him into a loft and tossed the rope over a stout overhead beam they knew would take his weight for sure. But when they pushed him from the loft, the rope snapped clean in two.

By that time, it was starting to seem like a big unfunny joke, and the lawmen felt like fools. They decided to get real serious and took the man to the next county where there was a federal prison and a proper gallows. They stood him on the platform, certain this time nothing could go wrong. But the trap wouldn't open. No matter what they did and how many times they tested it, when the man stood on that trapdoor, it just wouldn't open. A judge ruled that three times was all the chances you could decently have to hang a man, and let him go. So he walked out of the jail, a free man. And with his first steps, he tripped, fell off the sidewalk, and broke his neck.

Randy said that was a strange story, sure enough, and tried to match it with one of his own. He told him about a miner in Colorado—Pat Darcey, he thought the man's name was—who was famous throughout the territory as someone who found gold as easily as other men locate their boots in the morning. It just seemed to show up wherever he was.

Well, the story went that one time Darcey was at a funeral for one of his friends. He knelt down and picked up a handful of soil to drop on the coffin. But instead of tossing the dirt in the hole, he sifted it through his fingers and got real interested in it. Quietly, he stepped to the back of the crowd and started to mark a claim. The minister was the only one who could see what Darcey was up to, and he got so excited he could hardly finish the ceremony. The preacher wrapped it up quick with a prayer that ended, "So we say farewell to the dearly departed . . . and for Chrissakes, Pat, stake a claim for me! Amen."

Rule chuckled and said that was a pretty good yarn.

"Not bad," Randy said. Then he quietly added, "Even better since it's true. Not like your ol' Trooper story."

Rule looked at him and said, "Figured that out, did you?"

"Why'd you tell me that if it wasn't true?"

"Well, I just thought you'd enjoy hearing it. It was only a story, like the dime novels you read. Doesn't matter so much if it's true or not."

"I thought we was friends."

"We are friends," Rule said. "I enjoy your company more than anyone in a long time."

"Then why'd you lie to me? I thought friends always tell each other the truth."

Rule lowered his head and sighed. "No, not always," he said. "Truth isn't something you can pass back and forth, or even share. You have to decide it for yourself. And no two people—not even friends—will always agree on what that is."

Randy thought about that a moment. "My ma said that part of growin' up is learnin' that people and things aren't always what they first seem to be."

Rule nodded. "She's right about that."

"Does that include you?"

"Especially me," Rule said.

Randy peered at him real hard, but there wasn't a clue to what he meant, and Rule didn't offer to explain. "Why?" he asked finally. "What's the truth about you? What is there inside you that you don't show?"

"Nothing. I'm an exception. The exception to all rules is another Rule."

A thought was nagging at Randy, but he couldn't quite get it. "No, there is something you keep to yourself. . . . It's about McAllister, isn't it? Why do you hate him so much?"

Rule frowned. "You know all that."

"No, there's something more. Lots of men see their friends killed in wars. But they live with it. They don't go to the trouble for revenge you do."

Rule sighed. "You sure you want to know?"

Randy nodded firmly.

"All right." He turned in the saddle and stared straight ahead, his eyes focused far up the mountain, and he spoke almost as if he were saying it to himself. "You want to know why I hate McAllister and the other traitors? Because they showed me the truth. A truth inside me that I never suspected."

"I don't get what you're sayin'."

"That day at Whiteridge, while my friends were being murdered, you know what I did? I lay in the brush, and prayed they wouldn't spot me there. All those good men fell, and I didn't raise a hand to stop it."

"Yeah, but you were wounded."

"The wounds didn't stop me. It was only the fear. When my moment of truth came, I stuck my face in the mud and pretended to be dead. You understand what I'm telling you?"

"But there wasn't anything you could do against all those men," Randy protested.

"I could have got two or three of them before they got me. At least that would have been something. But I couldn't make myself do it. I found out what was inside me that day, what kind of man I truly am. There's all kinds of truth . . . and some of them, you're better off not knowing."

After that, the land began to get steep and rocky, so they had to concentrate on seeing that the horses didn't take a misstep. They didn't talk anymore for a long time, and in a strange way Randy was almost grateful.

"Mister, you come a long way for nothing, if mining's what you hoped to see," Ray Hodge said. "There's not enough work gettin' done here to make a man feel useful."

"Ain't it the truth?" Sam Cobb said around a mouthful of plug tobacco. "Shameful slow around here. And I'm not so happy about it, neither. Mrs. Cobb didn't raise no lazy son."

They had located the two line bosses without any search at all. They were sitting together outside the workmen's bunkhouse, rocking away what was left of the morning as if they didn't have a care in the world. Which seemed odd to Randy, since he knew Saturday was a workday. But there was hardly any activity in the camp at all. Besides Hodge and Cobb, there were only five or six other men around, and most of them were in the shack, still asleep, though it was nearly noon.

"Why is it so slow right now?" Rule asked them.

Hodge peered at Rule through a cloud of pipe smoke and shook his head. "I don't know if that's strictly your business, now, is it? What is it you're after, anyway, mister?"

"Just curious," Rule said.

"Well, curiosity killed the cat, you know, and it don't do much good for nosy strangers, either. If you take my drift."

Randy stepped in between the two men. "You can trust Rule, Mr. Hodge," he said. "My pa thinks real highly of him."

Cobb leaned forward and spat brown tobacco juice in the dust, then stared at Rule while he wiped his lips. "That so? Well, your pa's a good man, boy. I'm right sorry to hear he won't be comin' back to work with us. But seein' the state of things up here, maybe he's better off."

Randy glanced around at the almost empty camp. The question was a dreadful thing to think about, but it had to be asked. "You're not closin' down the mine, are you?"

"No, course not, just a slowdown is all," Cobb said. He looked at Hodge, who just shrugged. Cobb crooked a finger and motioned the boy closer. "But just between me and you, it's coming. Not now, but soon."

"Really?"

"It's not a thing I'd joke about."

Randy looked back and forth between the two crusty line bosses. "But why?"

Hodge tapped his pipe on the side of his chair, and said gruffly, "Only one reason to ever close down a mine, boy."

"You mean it's played out?"

"No, there's still silver to be took. Just ain't so much of it as a body would like. And what's there is all in hard rock, just ain't worth the effort to get it out. Even the high-grade pickings is lean."

"High-grade?" Rule asked. "What's that?"

Hodge laughed. "This topsider don't know much, does he?"

Randy looked back at Rule and explained, "High-gradin' is when a miner steals ore, sneaks it out in his pockets or in a toolbox or such. It's called high-grade 'cause they usually pick the best pieces for themselves."

"First sign of an ailin' mine," Hodge said, "is a miner at the end of a day with flat pockets. When you see 'em come outta the shaft with a springy step, you know times is hard."

Rule asked, "You mean the miners steal lumps of silver and you just let them get away with it?"

" 'Course we don't," Hodge said, grumbling around the stem of his pipe. "We stop 'em when we catch 'em. But these men have been at this work most of their lives, some of 'em since they was the age of this boy here. There's more tricks than you can shake a stick at, and they knows all of 'em."

Cobb said, "Ain't it the truth? You can't stop the stealing that goes on except by the dumb ones. But then, any man who chooses to live his whole life in a hole in the ground, how smart can he be? A good number of 'em don't really know what's worth stealing and what ain't."

"How's that?" Rule asked.

Hodge and Cobb grinned at each other, then at the boy. Cobb said, "Where'd you find this fella, son? He don't know a thing about silver, does he?"

"Only the kind he spends," Randy said. The line bosses laughed, but Rule didn't seem to find it so funny.

Hodge got to his feet and stretched, then motioned to Rule. "Come on over here, mister. You might as well learn something whilst you're here."

He strode away in the direction of the mine shaft. Rule shrugged, then he and Randy took off after him. Hodge was a game little bowlegged man, without an ounce of fat on him, and he moved nimbly over the rocks and scree as if there were nothing to it. Rule and Randy had to work to keep up.

He led them out of the camp, which was merely a few sheds made of rough-milled lumber, one for sleeping, a mess hall to eat in, and another for storing equipment and tools. Northcamp wasn't one of the better mining camps Randy had been in; it was still a pretty small operation. Besides the buildings for the men, and some more for the animals, there were only a few sluice boxes, long wooden troughs with rockers for sifting out gold.

Randy told Rule that sluices were more for placer mining than hard-rock mining, the sort done here, and they looked scarcely used. Gold often did show up in silver veins, he explained, sometimes the two were even bound together, but little had shown itself in this site.

The shaft was on a rocky ledge about ten feet above the gully in which the buildings had been erected. It didn't look like much on the outside, just a hole in the ground about eight feet square, with a wooden scaffold above it to support the hoists and pulleys that raised and lowered the miners in the shaft. Just to one side of the mine was a wide rock shelf, and it was on this natural platform that most of the ore brought up was piled, for grading and sorting, before being hauled away by mule-drawn wagons about every other week.

Hodge led them straight to the pile of ore, bent down, and picked up one lump of stone. He toyed with the rock up and down, hefting it as if it were a skipping stone and he was just looking for a pond to skim it across.

"Take a gander at this, Mr. Rule," Hodge said, once they had caught up to him. He tilted his head at the pile of stone. "There's silver in this lot, if you know what to look for. Think you can find it?"

Rule gazed over the mound of stones and shook his head. "It all looks like useless rock to me."

Randy picked up a lump of quartz with a faint greenish cast and handed it to him. "Here you go."

"Not bad, boy," Hodge said. "You have an eye on you."

Rule said, "It's not silver colored at all, is it? Does it always look this way?"

Hodge shook his head. "No such luck. Silver's a contrary metal, doesn't show itself the same way twice, sometimes has different appearances even in the same hole. Depends on what it bonds to. In parts of Colorado, where it mixes with lead, I seen it black as tar. Other places it can be yellow, brown, white, or red. Sometimes blue, when it's fused with gold. Nothing like that here, though, sorry to say."

Rule held the ore up to the light and squinted at it. "How can you be sure what you have is the real thing, then?"

"Only way to be sure is to have it tested," Hodge said. "That's done with hydrochloric and nitric acids, but them's too dangerous to haul through this rough country." He dumped his own rock back on the pile and sighed. "Silver never shows up in easy places. Takes a lot of capital to mine hard rock. Refining it ain't cheap, either. That's why it's a rich man's game. Gold's a lot more popular—it's easier on both the soul and the boot leather."

Rule stared at the ore in his hand, twisting it this way and that so that sunlight shimmered across it. "So you'd say the assayer is a pretty important man in the whole process?"

"He is that," Hodge said. "A good one can make you or break you. He's the only one who can be sure if you're making a fortune or just wasting your time."

"I suppose an unscrupulous assayer could find ample opportunities to make himself rich, couldn't he?"

Hodge nodded. "It's been known to happen. You ask me, they're all bandits, the fees they charge. But some's more crooked than others."

"How would a crooked one make his money?" Rule asked. "Undervalue the ore and then skim money off the top when it really sells at a higher price?"

"Well, maybe," Hodge said.

"That ain't the problem we got here," Cobb said, trailing up to rejoin them.

"What do you mean?" Rule asked.

"Cobb?" Hodge said, his voice pitched at a warning. "Mind yourself, now. Don't go shootin' off your mouth."

"Hell, there ain't no point in keepin' it to ourselves. This fella already knows there's something funny goin' on here. Do you think he come all this way for the view?"

The line boss turned to Rule and asked him straight out, "You're a lawman, ain't you?"

"That's right," Rule said. "With federal authority."

"I knew it," Cobb said. "Saw it right off."

"I still say it's no business to discuss with outsiders," Hodge grumbled.

Cobb shook his head at his friend. "You can tell from all the questions he's askin' about the assayer that he's got the same suspicions as us. The funny business with this mine ain't none of our doin'. What you want to protect them slick-suited shylocks for?"

"You mean McAllister, don't you?" Rule asked. "And Taggart. He's part of it, too, isn't he?"

Hodge scuffed at the dirt with his steel-toed boots. "Aw, go ahead and spill the beans, Cobb. You said too much to back off now."

Cobb took some time to think while he stuffed more tobacco in his cheek, then turned to face Rule. "It's like this, mister. I seen the assay results for myself, last time I was down at the development office. Wasn't supposed to see 'em, but I did. And the fact is, they was a pack of outright lies."

"How so?"

"Hell, those reports made it sound like we're workin' the biggest bonanza since the Comstock Lode. Accordin' to them assay results, we're supposed to be producin' near twelve hundred ounces to the ton. Now, I ain't no assayer, but I been scratchin' hard rock all my life, and I know we ain't doin' half that much."

"No way in the world," Hodge said.

"So Taggart and McAllister concocted false assay results to make this mine appear more productive than it really is. Why do you think they would do something like that?"

"Hell, don't have to think about it at all, do we?" Cobb said.

"It's clear as the nose on my face. Was all done to impress that other fella."

"What other fellow?"

"The one who was up here before you, earlier in the week. What was his name, Hodge? Coleman, was it? Colton, maybe?"

Hodge said, "Coleson. Nate Coleson." He blew through his pipe and made a sour face. "I can tell you, it wouldn't take much to impress that one. He hardly knew any more about silver than you do, mister."

"Taggart showed Coleson the mine? Why did he do that?"

Hodge and Cobb grinned at each other like they were dealing with the dumbest greenhorn they'd ever met. Cobb looked back at Rule and said, "Because Taggart wants the fella to buy it, that's why. Why else write up assay results that make your mine seem something it ain't, plus send away half your miners so as to make the work look easier than it is?"

"That's all the slowdown was for," Hodge explained. "Taggart sent half the men off to Catton City to make it appear the mine can be productive with only a fraction of the men it really takes. Makes it seem more attractive, you know."

Cobb broke back in, "It's an old trick, we seen it all before. First thing you do when you got an ailin' mine is try to sell it off to someone else, preferably to someone who don't know anything about the business. If'n you can't make him buy it outright, you maybe can get him to buy in for some big shares. Enough money to run off with, stake you somewhere else."

"Yeah, happens that way all the time," Hodge said. "We seen it more times than we care to remember, ain't we, Cobb?"

"Ain't it the truth?"

Rule frowned, turned a little, and stared off at the wagon ruts running down the mountainside. "What will happen to the town if Taggart dumps the mine and clears out like you expect?"

"Well, I expect it will dry up and blow away, like so many have before. Won't be any point to it with the mine shut down."

Cobb said, "Folks will just have to clear out, try again somewhere else. It's a hardship, but that's how it happens. The mining game's a gamble, and people in it are used to this kind of thing. Hell, even someone young as you has probably seen this a time or two, ain't you, boy?"

Randy nodded but didn't say anything. There was a lump in his throat that felt as big as one of the ore stones.

Hodge stepped up and put his hand under the boy's chin, tilted his head up and made him meet his eyes. "I trust you, son, to keep what you heard to yourself. No point in causin' a panic down there in Bannon, when it still could be that none of this will happen. The pickings is skimpy now, but could be there's enough to keep the mine open a spell longer. Things could turn around yet, you just never know."

"You too, mister," Cobb said to Rule. "We told you what we did in confidence. What we said is our suspicions, nothing more. So it's damned important you don't let out anything we said. Could cause one hell of a lot of trouble."

Rule said softly, "Even more than you know. You don't have to worry about us on that account."

"Yeah, we won't tell anyone," Randy added.

"You say your folks is already fixin' to leave town?" Hodge said to him. "That could be a good thing. No reason to hang around here no more."

"What will happen to you when this shuts down?" Rule asked the two men.

Hodge jammed his pipe back between his teeth and pointed off to the northwest, at the long run of mountains strung one after the other as far as the eye could see. "I got me half a mind to stay above ground from now on," he said. "Do something safe and sensible, like prospect gold. Cobb's fixin' to come in with me, too. Ain't you, Cobb?"

"Thinkin' on it," his friend said.

Hodge went on, "Yeah, pannin' color in a little stream out in the open air sounds like a decent way to live. I seen all the underbelly of these hills I care to. Life can't be no tougher on their topside. That's what I'm gonna do, mister. Stick to soft metal for a change."

"Prospecting's still pretty risky," Rule said. "That's what you consider safe and sensible?"

Hodge said, "Hell, it beats workin' for someone else, don't it? All the trouble I seen in this profession is 'cause of the people in it. Rock you can trust. It will kill you dead as a doornail, but only if you don't respect it. Rock won't turn on you, do something you never expect. But people will, and you take a fool chance whenever you try to trust one. Am I right, Cobb?"

The other line boss spat in the dust, then raised his head and stared hard at Rule and the boy. "Ain't it the truth?" he said. And this time, it almost sounded as though he hoped for an answer.

CHAPTER 17

THEY took their time going back down the mountain. Randy's mare got spooked every time its nose was pointed down a steep slope, and had to be coaxed along gently. The ground was the color of rust, chewed up soft from all the recent traffic, so they had to pick their way with caution. The trail snaked across rocky ledges with heart-wrenching drops near enough to spit over. Every now and then, the horses' hoofs would kick loose some rubble and start a small slide, one rock crashing into another, until a wave of stones went tumbling with the roar of a mountain stream.

Then the clatter would suddenly stop. Dead stillness. A long moment of unnerving silence as the stones flew off a ledge. Randy would hold his breath until he finally heard them smack bottom somewhere in the darkness far below. A hollow echo would ring out down the gullies and canyons for several heartbeats longer, and there was something reassuring about the sound, the way it would fade off slowly, without surprises.

The sun was low at their backs and their shadows stretched down the trail far ahead of them. The wind had a mournful pitch, sounding distant and lonely even as it stung their faces. Time passed slowly, or seemed to. But when the ground finally leveled off and they emerged in the foothills, Randy stared in the direction of the town and was surprised to see lights shining there. Somehow, the night seemed to have slipped by and got there ahead of them.

When Rule spoke it startled Randy as though he'd woken from a deep sleep. "You do know how important it is not to say a word about what you heard today?" he asked.

"I won't mention it to anyone. Not even my folks."

Rule shook his head. "No, your parents have to be told. They must understand what Taggart's up to. It's my fault, I got you into this. I never should have brought you along."

The boy's feelings were hurt. He thought he'd been helpful getting Hodge and Cobb to open up. "Well, okay," Randy mumbled. "If you're sure that's how you want it."

"This may be the last time we see each other," Rule said. "Your folks will have to clear out now, as soon as possible."

"Why?"

Rule looked over at him, and in his eyes there was genuine sadness. "You don't understand, do you? It's not safe for you around here anymore. My blundering has got us both in over our heads. Taggart is scheming to make a lot of money, and he's not about to let anything stand in his way. If he found out what we know he'd have us both killed."

Randy felt hair stand up on the back of his neck. "You really think so?"

"I wouldn't care to gamble on it. Your folks have to get you out of here. Pack up, go away, and don't look back."

"What about you? What will you do?"

Rule sighed. "I have to try to stop him."

"But then he'll come after you."

"He may try. If he does, I'll be ready." Rule reined in his horse, leaned from the saddle, and stuck out his hand. "This is good-bye, Mr. Callum. I want you to ride on alone from here. It's best we don't be seen together anymore."

Randy shook his hand in a daze. His head was spinning with confusion, and his eyes were blurry from welling tears. "I don't want to say good-bye," he blurted.

"Me neither. But we have no choice." Then, in a firmer voice, Rule said, "Now go."

He slapped Randy's mare on the flank and she took off in a gallop. The boy held on, his face pressed to the horse's mane, and didn't try to stop her. He tried instead, to wipe the damp from his eyes. They weren't real tears, he thought, they couldn't be. Must be the sting of the wind and grit from the trail.

The horse kept running without any urging, as though it already smelled home. By the time Randy got his eyes cleared he was well down the hill. He looked back over his shoulder at the spot on the hillside where he'd left Rule. Rule was still there, he knew, but against the dark of the trees, his form was impossible to make out. It was as if he were already gone.

At the outskirts of town Randy climbed off the mare to walk her in the rest of the way. The horse needed to cool down after her run, and he wanted time to think. How could he break the news to his parents about the trouble he was in? That because of him they would have to leave their home, everything they'd worked for, and run off like scared rabbits. Randy wouldn't blame them if they never spoke to him again. Things had sure turned sour.

There was never a time when he'd felt so lost and all alone. He wished he could pretend the whole thing had never happened, that he'd never met Ulysses Rule at all, that he could just go back to being a kid, with no worries. . . .

But wishes wouldn't change anything. It was a sorrowful fact, but one he had come to learn and accept. Maybe he had grown up a little. But it wasn't something he was pleased about. Not if growing up meant learning to live with regrets.

With such thoughts filling his head, he was well into town before it struck him that something wasn't quite right there. Bannon was always a quiet town, but things were *too* quiet. Randy realized he hadn't seen a single soul anywhere among the outlying homes and shops. Evenings were a peaceful time, but also when folks went visiting—it seemed downright unnatural for them all to be shut in.

He stopped and looked around. Most of the buildings looked empty and dark. Then he cocked his head, listening hard. After a moment the sound came to him, a low murmur, a hum, barely audible above the steady wail of the wind.

It was a sound he had heard once before. He gave the mare's reins a yank and moved off faster, worried now.

The sound got louder closer to the center of town, and Randy had a suspicion of what he'd find when he got there, but not why. It was the noise of many voices all chattering at once, excited voices. Something big must have happened while he was away, something big enough to stir a crowd.

Sure enough, he turned onto the main street near the saloon, and there they all were, mobs of people all jammed together in one spot. Nearly the whole town was gathered outside Murtry's feed store. Townsfolk were standing around in a wide circle, and at the heart of that circle were about twenty men on horseback. Taggart was among them, and his men made up most of the riders. Every one of them was packing a rifle or a pistol.

Randy looked toward the feed store then, and saw Murtry standing on the sidewalk with the Sharps cradled in his arms. His head was wrapped in a white bandage. His face had a grim and determined look. As Randy watched, Earl Vickers came out from the general store carrying a whole armload of rifle cartridges. Murtry barked an order to him, and Vickers began passing out shells to all the riders.

A small commotion caught Randy's attention, and he turned to see his mother pushing and shoving her way to him through the crowd. She barged up and crushed him in a hug that nearly forced the air out of him. "Randy! Thank God you're safe. I was so worried."

He felt dampness on his cheek and pushed her away a little, gently, until he could see her face. Tears were streaming from her eyes. "Ma? What is it? What's goin' on?"

She smothered him with another hug, then anger suddenly flickered in her eyes. "I knew it was wrong to let you go with that man. I can't believe I did such a stupid thing!"

"I'm fine, Ma. Really."

Sarah glanced aside at all the activity and made a sour face. "Useless men in this town—they stand around all day talking, waiting for the sheriff to get his head mended and his wits together. It's not until nightfall, once they get a few drinks inside them, that any of them gets up the gumption to actually do something."

"Do *what?*" Randy asked.

She grabbed his hand and started dragging him through the crowd. "Come on. We have to find your father before he runs off with those gun-crazy fools."

Randy gave up and let himself be steered along. She pushed through the people like a madwoman, waving her free hand in the air and yelling her husband's name. A second later she spotted him leading a horse saddled and loaded with gear for a ride of several days. "Dan," she cried. "Look!"

A second later Callum had his arms around Randy and he was having the wind squeezed out of his lungs again.

Then Callum backed off, embarrassed by his public display. He grinned and tussled Randy's hair. "Sure glad to see you, son. We nearly had the wits scared out of us."

"That's putting it mildly," Sarah said.

Randy frowned. "Would someone kindly tell me what's goin' on? Why are these people here? What's all the fuss about?"

His father said, "They're forming a posse. Didn't you hear?"

"Hear what? I only this minute got back in—"

Just then, someone in the crowd yelled, "Look, there he is!"

Everybody turned all at once and stared up the street. Randy stretched up on his toes to see over all the heads and could just make out the figure of a lone rider on a big black horse.

Callum let out a little whistle under his breath, and muttered, "He came back. I'd never believe it if I didn't see it with my own eyes."

"What are you talking about?" Randy said. "It's just Rule."

Sarah's grip tightened on the boy's hand. "Come on," she said sternly. "Let's get out of here."

"No, wait," Randy protested, and there was no pleading in his voice at all. He didn't mean to be moved.

Rule rode in slowly, looking neither left nor right. His face was calm and composed, showing no surprise at the unexpected gathering. The crowd gave way, and then swarmed up behind him, following closely.

He rode straight past the group of riders until he came face to face with Taggart. Even then, Rule didn't let out a flicker of what he felt. Taggart, though, wore a smile from ear to ear.

"Well, well. I'm surprised to see you again, hangman. You don't have half the brains I gave you credit for."

Greene snickered by his boss's shoulder. "Yeah, let's see you talk your way outta this one."

Rule didn't bat an eye. He reined his horse past those two and rode on until he came to the feed store. Murtry stood there, looking glum.

"Evening, Sheriff," Rule said. "What's that on your head? You run into something?"

Murtry stepped to the edge of the sidewalk and spoke in a tone both sad and grimly serious. "Mr. Rule, step down from your horse, sir."

"Mind telling me what for?"

"Just get down," Murtry insisted.

Rule sighed. "Whatever you say." Slowly, he swung down from his horse and stood face to face with the sheriff. They locked eyes for a long moment.

"Your weapons," Murtry demanded. "Bring that shotgun out nice and easy."

"I hope you have a good explanation for this." With one hand, Rule reached under his cloak. A gasp went through the crowd when the mean-looking sawed-off 12-gauge flashed into view.

Two men pounced on him from either side. One took the

shotgun away, the other snatched the revolver from his holster.

"And the wrist gun," Murtry said to the deputies. "There's a knife in his boot. Get that, too. Search him over good."

The two men patted Rule down from head to toe. He tolerated their hands in silence, never once taking his eyes off Murtry. Then the two men stepped back.

"That's it. He's clean," one of them announced.

"I'm still waiting," Rule said to the sheriff.

Murtry stepped down from the sidewalk and took a long deep breath. "You want an explanation?" he said. He motioned again to the two men. They moved up and grabbed Rule's arms. "Okay, here it is. Ulysses Rule, I hereby arrest you for the murder of Tom McAllister."

CHAPTER 18

"ARE you telling me McAllister's dead?"

"That's the size of it," Murtry said. "Found him late this morning, hangin' from a beam, neck snapped like a twig."

"And you figure I did it?"

Murtry nodded. "It was your rope. Fancy piece of braid-work, can't be many like it in this town."

"The rope I left in my room. Anyone could have broken in and taken it."

"Well, that's your story. I can't say it impresses me much."

"Why would I kill him now? It doesn't make any sense."

"It's no secret how bad you hated McAllister. Didn't count on the marshals to send a judge, did you? You thought they'd say to go ahead and string him up. Only they didn't do that. A judge was bad news for you, a judge might decide either way. So you made up your mind not to wait."

"Got it all figured out, don't you?" Rule said. "But I couldn't have done it. I haven't been around here all day."

"No? Where were you then?"

"Up to the mine."

Taggart flinched so hard his horse reared and almost bucked him off. His eyes got big and his face turned red. "You did what!"

Rule turned his way, smiling faintly. "Interesting place. I learned all kinds of things I didn't know before."

"That mine is private property! Nobody invited you up there. Nosy, insolent bastard, interfering in my affairs. By God, I'll have you horsewhipped!"

Rule shrugged and looked back to Murtry. "Is that part of the plan, Sheriff?"

"It's a point in your defense, if you were really up there like you say." Murtry spoke to Rule, but while he did, his eyes searched through the crowd, and stopped when they lit on Randy. "Is there anyone who can back up your claim?"

"No, I went alone."

"There, you see?" Taggart said. "He can't prove a thing. It's all lies." A murmur of agreement rose from the crowd.

"Too bad," Murtry said, shaking his head. The sheriff's gaze stayed on Randy a moment longer, then he gestured to the men holding Rule. "But I promise to look into it. You'll have a chance to make your case soon as the trial starts."

One deputized posseman gave Rule a rough shove in the back to start him toward the jail. But Taggart spurred his horse up to block their way. "Hold on, Sheriff," he growled. "You're not taking him anywhere."

Murtry scowled at Taggart. "What's that you say?"

Taggart stood up in the stirrups so everyone could see him. He spoke to Murtry, but it was really the crowd he was addressing, trying to whip them up. "Tom McAllister was one of our own," he said. "A respected figure in our community. But now he's gone, taken from us. One of our own, savagely murdered. Someone's got to pay for that."

"It's up to the law to decide that," Murtry said.

"Where was the law when this man killed Tom? Where were you, Sheriff?"

Another murmur sounded from the crowd. One man yelled out, "That's tellin' him!"

Murtry grumbled, "You got something against me, Taggart, come out and say it."

"Not plain enough for you? All right, I'll spell it out for you. I say we don't have any law in this town, all we have is an incompetent old coot with a badge. We're all supposed to look to you for protection, Murtry. But you couldn't even protect a man in your own jail."

"Yeah, that's right," someone yelled. "Hell with the law. We

THE MEASURE OF JUSTICE ■ 155

know Rule killed him. I say we string him up now, and have done with it!"

Then Murtry did a funny thing. He laughed. He looked right at the man who yelled, tipped back his head and let out a barking laugh.

"What's so damned humorous," Taggart demanded.

"You are," Murtry said. "It's no trick to see through your schemin' ways. You paid that man to say those things, did you? Try to stir folks up, get 'em excited, maybe rouse a lynchin'?"

"It's what he deserves. This town demands justice. If you won't do the right thing, we'll see to the matter ourselves."

"You wouldn't know the right thing if it bit you on the butt," Murtry said. "These people aren't gonna lynch anybody. They don't give a damn about justice, they don't give a damn about anything but their own selves. They let you tell 'em what to think for so long, they can't put two thoughts together on their own without bustin' a gut."

Taggart spun around in the saddle and started to address the crowd again, "Are you going to leave justice to the likes of him? I say we take matters into our own hands and—"

Murtry reached up, real slow, grabbed a handful of Taggart's waistcoat, and dragged him off his horse, then stared him down nose to nose.

Taggart's eyes grew round. "What the hell are you playing at?" he mumbled.

"Now you're gonna listen to me," Murtry said. "You might own this town, but you can't buy this man's life. For once, we're gonna see things done right. There's a federal judge already on his way here. He will decide the facts in this matter. Not you."

"You idiot. The judge was supposed to rule about the charges against Tom. But now he's dead."

Murtry said calmly, "That's right. Whatever Tom did or didn't do doesn't matter anymore. But now we got us a murder. The evidence seems to point to Rule here, so I'll hold him. Hold him until the judge arrives and we can have a trial. You claim you want justice, Taggart? That's just what we'll have, the real law-and-order kind, not the sort you can buy and sell."

Taggart was shaking like a mad dog on a short leash. "Watch your mouth, Murtry. I mean to avenge Tom, and we'll walk right over you if we have to."

"Taggart, I don't think you want to cross me." There was menace in Murtry's voice, and a quiet strength no one had ever suspected in him before.

"You wouldn't dare stop me."

Murtry shrugged. "Well, maybe I would and maybe I wouldn't, who knows? Kinda curious, myself. There's one way to find out."

No one in the crowd breathed for nearly a whole minute. The silence was so deep Randy could hear his own heart pound.

Finally, Taggart hissed, "Damn you, old man." With that, he spun on his heel, grabbed the reins of his horse, and savagely yanked its head around. He stormed off through the crowd, and a good number of them, his men, trailed away behind him.

Murtry gave Rule a half smile, then the two deputies hustled him inside the jail. Murtry hollered out to the rest of the people still milling around, "That's it. Go on back home. Or wherever the hell you want to . . . just go away."

And the crowd did what he said. People had seen Murtry face down Taggart, and they listened to him with a newfound respect. Whatever else came from the whole sorry business, Sheriff Murtry had found himself.

Randy told his parents that they would have to leave town, and watched them each react to the news in a different way. His father stood by the window, back stiff and straight, a tight look of concern on his face, and got real quiet. Which was fine, since Sarah did enough talking for both of them. Randy was afraid his mother would cry, but she didn't. His parents' reactions swung wildly between fear, sad resignation, and a deep, seething anger.

"I can't believe it," Sarah said. "It's just too incredible. Why would Taggart do such a thing?"

"To get rich," Randy said simply.

"He wouldn't sell us all out. He couldn't. He brought us all together in the first place. He guided us, inspired us. We *believed* in him."

Callum said gently, "We believed in ourselves, Sarah. All Taggart did was figure a way to profit from our dreams."

She looked at him. "Dan, you really think he sold us out?"

"If Cobb and Hodge think so, then I do, too."

"We invested so much in this place. Everything we had, all our savings, all our hopes."

Callum shook his head. "All gone."

"No, I won't accept that. I can't."

"Sarah, get hold of yourself."

"Don't tell me what to do," she snapped. "It's your fault we're in this trouble. We never should have let Randy go with that terrible man. I only said it was all right because I knew you wanted it."

"Rule didn't create this trouble, he just brought it to light. We can't blame him for our mistakes."

Her head came up. "Can't I? Nothing like this happened until he came around. Now they say he murdered that poor man in the jail. I hope Rule swings for it, I really do. I want to see them string him up from the gallows he paid to build."

"Sarah, you don't mean that."

She glared at him defiantly. "I do. So help me, I do."

Randy put a hand on her arm and said, "Ma, I told you. Rule couldn't have done it. He was with me the time they say McAllister was killed. By then we were already well on our way to the mine."

"No, he did it. Somehow, I don't know how, but he was responsible. A man like that will stop at nothing to get what he wants. He found a way."

"Ma, no. I tell you it's not true."

She shook off Randy's hand. "Everyone says he's guilty."

Callum said softly, "Sarah, listen to yourself. You accept gossip and rumors over the word of your own son?"

"I just know what I feel. And I don't trust Rule. I never have. He's done nothing but bring us trouble."

"He's not like that," Randy said. "Ma, you heard him lie to protect me."

"Lies come easy to that sort of man," she said.

Randy frowned, getting angry. "He could have saved himself, but he didn't. Only 'cause he was scared for me. Now they're gonna put him on trial for something he didn't do. And I got to help him."

Callum said gently, "I know, son. But there's nothing you can do for him now."

"There is. I have to speak up for him at the trial, tell everyone the truth."

Sarah looked sharply at her husband. Callum shook his head. "No, boy. I can't let you do that."

"But—"

"No. That's final. Rule knew what he was doing. It's not safe for you here. We move on before any trial."

"We can't just run off and leave him."

"I don't like it any more than you. But we don't have a choice. Rule's on his own now, and so are we. We leave town just as soon as we can."

Sarah hung her head. She looked as though she was finally going to cry, but still the tears wouldn't come. "All gone," she said under her breath. "Everything . . . all gone."

Callum put his hands on her shoulders. "We'll make a clean start somewhere new," he said. "We've done it before. At least we'll still be together."

Sarah swallowed hard and looked up at him. "There must be some way, some other way . . . if only we could—"

Callum touched a finger to her lips and shushed her gently. "I'll start building some crates to pack our things in."

CHAPTER 19

THE next couple days were tense for Randy, but not as fearful as he expected. He thought he should feel different with a death threat hanging over his head, but somehow he didn't. Even his parents relaxed a little when it became apparent that Taggart didn't know they were onto his scheme. But they still planned to move out as soon as they could.

Randy's father worked out a deal with Mr. Lawrence at the general store to build some shelves in exchange for all the groceries he had purchased on credit. He labored practically day and night to get them done so they could leave. With Randy's help the job would have gone faster, but Callum wanted the boy to stay out of sight as much as possible.

In fact, Randy's parents hardly let him out of the house; they wanted him with one of them every minute, and it was almost like being in jail. The time wasn't idle, though. He had to help his mother decide what things to keep and what things to leave, then pack it all up into one tight wagonload. Randy was surprised how difficult that chore turned out to be; they had accumulated a lot of odds and ends in the time since they had settled in Bannon. He never knew one family could own so much stuff.

On Monday morning a buckboard wheeled into town carrying the Honorable Warren Timmons. He was given the best room in the hotel and one day to rest from his trip before the trial. It was announced that the proceedings would commence Tuesday morning in the new Union Hall, the building Callum had completed only the week before. So much had happened in that week, to Randy it seemed a lifetime ago instead of only a few days.

Randy's father had an announcement of his own: Over supper that night, he told his family that the job at the general store would be finished by noon the next day. Shortly after lunchtime tomorrow, he said, they would climb on their wagon and leave Bannon for good. After that they finished their meal in silence, all knowing it was the last supper they would have in that house. It was a somber thought, and Randy felt especially sad, because he figured it was all his fault.

They had just finished clearing away the dishes when there came a knock on the door. Randy nearly jumped out of his skin. First ordering Sarah and Randy to stay out of sight, Callum went to the door and pulled it open. Outside stood a smallish young man in a costly wool suit, with big round spectacles that gave him sort of an owlish look. He smiled in a friendly way and stuck out his hand.

"Daniel Callum? Sorry to disturb your evening, sir, but I would like a word with you, if you don't mind."

"Who're you?" Callum asked.

He handed over a small white card bearing the elaborately scrolled words *Nelson Winslow, Attorney at Law*. "Mr. Callum, I have agreed to represent Ulysses Rule. Do you mind if I come in? Considering the circumstances, it might be best if we spoke privately."

Callum nodded and ushered him inside. He led the young man through the sitting room, which was almost bare except for a few boxes and bundles ready to be loaded on the wagon the next day. "Packing up, I see," Winslow said. "I hope I can convince you to delay your departure for a few more days."

"How's that?" Callum grumbled.

Then they came around to the kitchen, where Winslow spotted Randy and Sarah. The lawyer's boyish face split in a wide grin. "Ah, this must be Randall. I've heard good things about you."

"You have?" Randy said.

"I certainly did. My client speaks very highly of you."

Sarah stepped forward and said, "In this house, sir, *your client's* opinion is not held in any high regard."

Winslow's owlish smile didn't flicker. "I'm sorry to hear that, ma'am. Mr. Rule seems impressed by all of you, in fact. He described you as a most charming family."

Callum pulled out two chairs from the kitchen table and motioned for the young man to sit. He said gruffly, "Why don't you dispense with the flattery and tell us what it is you want?"

Winslow took off his spectacles and began polishing them with a handkerchief. "I should think that is obvious, sir. I have come in the hopes of persuading you to let your son testify tomorrow."

"Then you're wasting your time."

"I knew it!" Sarah exploded. Winslow glanced over at her and raised an eyebrow in puzzlement. She went on, "I knew Rule couldn't be trusted. He promised Randy wouldn't have to be involved. The trial's not even started yet, and already he's gone back on his word. The man only cares about himself."

"I think I should explain something," Winslow said. "By coming here tonight I have directly violated the wishes of my client. Mr. Rule expressly forbade me to speak to any of you. With all due respect, ma'am, I can assure you that the welfare of your son is his foremost concern."

"So you say," Sarah muttered. But some of the fight had gone out of her. She dropped wearily into a chair. "If that's true, then what are you doing here?"

"I want to see justice done." Winslow looked back and forth between Dan and Sarah. "It should be clear to both of you from what your son has said that Mr. Rule could not have committed the murder he is accused of. But there is circumstantial evidence which will weigh heavily against him. And sentiment of the townspeople, in general, will not work in his favor."

"That's a fact." Callum sighed. "He didn't exactly make himself popular. I heard folks talkin' at the store all day. Sounds like the whole town's got it in for him."

Winslow nodded. "Your son's testimony is his only chance. Randall is the only person who can swear to Rule's whereabouts at the time the murder occurred. You must see your way to let him come forward."

"To save Rule?"

"Yes," Winslow said. "To save an innocent man."

Callum shook his head. "Then who will save *Randy* once he's done that? *You*, Mr. Winslow? What can your laws and fancy talk do to protect my boy? You must be pretty green if you think a matter like this ends in a courtroom. How long do you think Randy would live after he gave witness against Taggart?"

"Mr. Taggart would gain nothing by causing harm to your son. I understand your concern, but—"

"Gain?" Callum said, cutting the lawyer off short. "The point is what would he stand to *lose*? Let's speak plainly, Mr. Attorney, no beatin' round the bush. If my son proves Rule innocent he'll also be pointing a finger at the one who's really guilty."

"That's true, I suppose," Winslow admitted. "With Rule exonerated, suspicion would naturally fall on the one we know is truly responsible."

"No supposin' about it," Callum snapped. "You put Randy on a witness stand, you're not gonna leave it at where Rule was and when. You'll make him tell *everything* he knows. All about Taggart's plans to sell out the mine, why that gave him a motive to kill McAllister before the scandal came out and scared off the syndicate money. You'll make certain it all comes out, the whole story, won't you? That's your job."

"All right." Winslow sighed. "You're correct. I would do

my best to stop short of making outright accusations. But if pressed, I would have no choice but to make sure Randy casts suspicion where it rightly belongs."

Sarah came around the table and threw her arms around Randy. "You might as well just put a gun to my son's head," she said.

"Madam, I assure you, the law —"

Callum slammed his fist down on the table so hard the top nearly split. The lawyer shut his mouth quickly.

"No," Callum declared. "That is my answer to you. I don't know where you come from, mister, but around here the law isn't worth more than spit in the river. Men like Taggart don't care about what's right and what's wrong—only about gettin' even."

"Rule got himself into this," Sarah said. "He can get himself out."

"We are talking about saving a man's life. If Rule is convicted, he'll be hanged. Your son is the only person who can prevent that."

"What about someone from the mine?" Callum asked. "Can't you get Hodge or Cobb to say what time Rule got there, how long he stayed?"

The lawyer shook his head. "The two men Rule spoke to have disappeared. None of the other miners seem to know what is going on, or if they do they won't admit to it."

Callum looked up. "Disappeared how?"

"I don't know, sir. They spoke to Mr. Rule about a desire to go prospecting for gold. Perhaps they decided not to wait any longer. Anyway, I hope that is the explanation for their absence."

"What do you mean—*you hope*?"

"We can't dismiss the possibility that their disappearance was not voluntary. Taggart may somehow have learned of their suspicions and taken steps to guarantee that they will not repeat them in court."

Sarah sat down again, heavily. "Those two kindly old men?" She buried her face in her hands.

Winslow glanced at her, then turned back to Callum, and the lawyer's eyes looked grim behind the shiny spectacles. "You understand exactly what I'm telling you? Even if he doesn't testify, your son represents a grave threat to Taggart. There is no telling how far he may go to eliminate that threat, should he ever learn of it."

Callum stood up quickly. "All the more reason to get out as fast as we can. I thank you for the warning, but Taggart has nothing to fear from us. Randy is not going to speak in that court, and that's my final word on it."

"I beg you one last time to reconsider. Rule needs your help. If you tie my hands, I'm not sure I can save him. Are you sure you can live with that on your conscience?"

Sarah looked over at the lawyer and said softly, "I have only one son. I can live with a stain on my conscience a lot easier than I can live without him."

Winslow nodded sadly and got to his feet. "Thank you for your time."

When the lawyer was halfway out of the room, Callum raised his head and said suddenly, "You can't win, you know. Men like Taggart always get their way. You can't beat 'em."

Winslow stopped and glanced back. "Maybe not. But I'll give him a good fight. That stands for something."

"For what? What's the point, if it's all useless anyway?"

Winslow smiled, but it was sort of a sad look. "Taggart may win—but we won't *lose*. Not the way you have. Good night to you."

Nobody answered him. After a moment, the lawyer turned away and quietly let himself out. Randy's parents sat staring at each other, but not saying a word. They looked stricken, like people at a graveside, full of grief and mourning over someone, or something, they never thought they'd say good-bye to.

*   *   *

Tuesday morning the Callum family rose early. None of them had slept much anyway. Sarah and Randy loaded the last of their belongings on the wagon while Callum went down to the general store to finish his work for Mr. Lawrence. There'd been a hard frost during the night and Sarah's flowers had withered. She stood by the fence a long time, her back to Randy, and when finally she turned around he saw her eyes were red and swollen. She closed up the house without a word, and they rode downtown.

They had been parked outside the store for only a minute when, across the way, the sheriff came out with two other men, both armed to the teeth. Murtry glanced up and down the street, then motioned to someone inside. Rule came out slowly, his hands manacled. The lawyer Winslow was with him. Randy tried to catch Rule's eye, but he never looked his way. The two deputies fell in on either side, and the group started off.

Randy noticed then how empty the town seemed; the whole place looked shut up and abandoned. It felt downright creepy being the only people in sight, and he said so to his mother. She nodded as if she had been feeling the same way. "Maybe we'll go inside and check on your father," she suggested.

So he helped her down and they went into the store. Groceries and dry goods were piled in the middle of the floor to make room while Callum added new shelves that ran the whole length of the room. Mr. Lawrence smiled and tipped his visor to Sarah. "Morning, ma'am. On your way to the trial, are you? You're late—whole town's down there already. Bet there's not a good seat left."

"Yes, you're probably right," Sarah said.

Mr. Lawrence peeled off his apron and visor, laid them out on the counter. "Just on my way down there, myself," he said. "Wouldn't want to miss it. Doin's like this don't come along every day. Well, maybe I'll see you there."

He came out from behind the counter, headed for the

door, then stopped and looked back around. "I was truly sorry to hear about you folks leavin' town. Don't suppose there's any chance you'd change your mind?"

"No, I don't think so," Sarah said, and the sadness in her voice was a sorry thing to hear.

"Too bad. We'll miss you folks round here. Well, I better git, else I'll wind up sitting in the street. Good luck to you, ma'am."

He turned and beat it out the door, moving smartly. The minute they were alone, Callum set down his tools and came over to his family.

"Taggart was just in here a bit ago. Buyin' cigars—to celebrate with," he said. "He was cocky and full of himself, braggin' how fast the trial was going to go. 'We'll have him strung up by sundown,' he claimed."

Sarah's eyes lit up with relief. "Then he couldn't suspect what Randy knows."

"No, I'm pretty sure he doesn't. We're almost home free. I just need a couple hours to finish here, then we will be on our way."

Sarah said, "So long? What do we do with ourselves in the meantime?"

Randy spoke up, "Let's go to the trial, Ma."

She frowned at him. "Now, son. You know we can't—"

"What's to stop us? Pa said Taggart doesn't suspect anything. Seems to me folks will wonder why we're not there along with everyone else."

She nodded thoughtfully and looked at her husband. "What do you think, Dan? He does have a point." Randy knew then she wanted to go as badly as he did and his hopes swelled. "Nothing could happen in front of all those people," she added.

"Please, Pa?" Randy said. "It would be terrible to leave town and never know what happened."

"Dan, I think it will be all right," Sarah said. "We'll sit at the back and not say a word. Hardly anyone will know we're there."

Randy cringed, for that was the opposite of what she'd just argued. But his father didn't seem to notice. "All right." He sighed. "I know how bad curiosity is eatin' you both up. But be careful and don't call attention to yourselves. Do what your mother tells you, boy, and no matter what you hear or see in that courtroom, you don't say a word. Is that clear?"

"Yessir," Randy said. It was all he could do to keep from shouting with relief. "I promise."

"And when I'm done here, we move on like we planned. No complaints. No matter how the trial goes, or how bad you want to know the outcome, when the time comes, we go. Agreed?"

"Sure, Pa. You know what's best."

Sarah nodded her consent as well.

"I hope so, son," Callum said. "Go on now, both of you, before I change my mind."

Sarah and her son looked at each other, and before Callum could pick up his hammer, they were out the door.

CHAPTER 20

THE crowd at the trial overflowed the Union Hall. Almost every chair inside was already taken, and the entrance was jammed with those folks more partial to breathing, who bunched outside the doorway where they could still hear and see.

The Union Hall had been built to accommodate both meetings and dances, though no such gatherings had been held as yet. There was a raised platform at the far end meant for the musicians, and for the trial they had placed on it one big desk, and a single hard chair for the witnesses. Earl Vickers from the bank was acting as court secretary, and was seated near the judge, where he could hear and jot down all that was said. Facing the judge were two tables, one on either side. Rule and Winslow were sitting at the one on the right, talking softly, Murtry and his deputies close behind. At the other table was Taggart, next to a tall, distinguished-looking gent with wavy black hair.

Randy and Sarah pushed their way inside and lucked upon two of the last chairs not taken in the very back row. Randy sat down next to his friend Bill Kitson.

"Come to see yer fancy-pants friend get his goose cooked, did ya?" Bill said with a cackling laugh.

Sarah patted Randy's knee and shook her head in a warning. She needn't have. Randy didn't have any idea what to say to him. He was spared from any more of Bill's remarks, for right then Earl Vickers called out, "Everybody stand."

The whole crowd got to their feet. Sunlight spilled through a door near the stage, then the judge came through it, looking smart and important in a long black robe. He was a

168

largish man, with a fleshy face ringed by gray hair—what there was left of it—and a neatly clipped goatee to steer the eye from what was missing.

The crowd stood in respectful silence, then the judge pounded on his desk with a gavel. "I declare this court in session," he said in a deep, clear voice. "Let's get this thing started."

There was a pause then while everyone looked around, wondering what came next. "Sit down," Vickers barked.

The rustle of chairs as everyone resettled themselves drowned out whatever he said next, then the judge took over again. He looked over all the faces and said, "In the interest of fast and fair justice—and because I have no desire to repeat a wearisome journey anytime soon—we will dispense with the formality of a hearing and proceed directly with the trial."

Winslow shot to his feet. "Your Honor, I protest."

The judge sighed and raised his eyebrows. "You are, sir?"

"Nelson Winslow, Your Honor. Representing the defense. I wish to raise a formal objection against the disregard for normal procedure in this instance."

"Your complaint is duly noted. Now, shall we begin?"

"If it would please the court—"

The judge cut him off with a smack of his gavel. "What would please this court, Mr. Winslow, is if we could just get on with it. Or do you intend to interrupt me every five seconds?"

"Your Honor, my client deserves the full protection of—"

"What your client deserves or doesn't deserve is exactly what we have gathered here to determine," the judge said. "And that determination will be made by me. Unless you wish to demand a trial by jury?"

Winslow shook his head. "In this town? No, sir."

"Then let us proceed. I gave my consent—somewhat generously, if I do say so myself—to preside over this trial even though it is not the matter for which I was originally summoned. Be that as it may, I am here *now*. And since I can assure you that no power on earth will drag me across those wretched mountains again anytime in the near future, *now* is when this case will be heard. Today, Mr. Winslow. Further delays will win you no sympathy from me. Do I make myself quite clear?"

The distinguished-looking man next to Taggart stood up then, and spoke out in a rich bass voice. "Your Honor, if I may interject?"

The judge turned to him. "Yes, what is it?"

"Deighton Kirby, Your Honor. For the prosecution."

The judge's voice turned pleased and respectful. "The court is well aware of your exemplary reputation, Mr. Kirby, and is honored by your presence here today."

"Thank you, Your Honor." Kirby aimed a sly smile in Winslow's direction before addressing the judge again. "May it please the court, the prosecution is fully ready . . . and *willing* to proceed."

The judge sighed. "Finally. That's more like it. An admirable and much appreciated suggestion, Mr. Kirby. Please call your first witness."

Kirby hooked his thumbs in the pockets of his red waistcoat and paced slowly back and forth across the front of the room. His booming voice rang out clear and true, so even people out in the street could hear him. "Now, Sheriff," the lawyer said. "Suppose you tell the court in your own words what happened on the morning in question."

Murtry stared out at the crowd from the witness chair, gave his head one quick polish, carefully avoiding the swollen spot near his left ear. "Well, I woke early, before sunrise, must of been. I got up and started bangin' around in the dark. I bruised my knee something awful on the table leg. Swelled up like a melon, see? Right here . . . But I suppose you don't care about that."

"Did something disturb your sleep, Sheriff?"

Murtry shrugged. "You might say that. Someone was pounding on my door like he was tryin' to break it down."

"And what did you do then?"

"I did what any man would do," Murtry said. "I went over and opened the door. Maybe it wasn't the smartest thing I ever done, but hell, no man thinks straight when he's spooked out of a sound sleep. And I've had little enough of that lately, standing guard day and night, never gettin' any decent rest. Watchin' over a prisoner ain't as easy as it sounds, you know."

Winslow spoke up from his chair. "Your Honor, please instruct the witness to stick to the point."

"Sustained," the judge said. He leaned over to look at Murtry. "We all appreciate the difficulties of your job, Sheriff. Try to restrict your comments to only the relevant facts."

Murtry frowned. "My sleep seemed plenty relevant to me at the time."

That got a laugh from the crowd, but Kirby moved back in before the judge could even raise his hammer. "You have our sympathies. Please tell us what happened after you opened the door."

"There wasn't anybody there," Murtry said. "For a minute I thought some kids had played a trick on me—you know, banged on my door and run off. But then I realized it was way too early in the morning for kids to be playing. Besides, there *was* somebody out there, I sensed that."

Kirby spoke up. "You sensed the presence of someone outside? What do you mean, Sheriff? *How* did you detect this person?"

"Well, I smelled him."

"What specifically did you smell?" Kirby moved even closer. "Tell us, Sheriff. Exactly what did you smell?"

Murtry hesitated and his eyes drifted in Rule's direction. "Pipe smoke," he said finally. "I smelled pipe smoke."

"And what did you do then?"

"I poked my head outside some more and looked around.

And then I saw him in the shadows down the boardwalk a ways."

Kirby leaned forward intently. The lawyer's body quivered like a taut bowstring. "Who did you see?"

"It was dark," Murtry said. "And I told you, he was back in the shadows, out of the moonlight. Hard to say who it was, exactly. I don't know for sure."

"Did this man speak to you?" Kirby asked. Murtry shook his head. "But you spoke to him, didn't you, Sheriff? Tell us what you said to this man who lured you outside so mysteriously."

Murtry drew in a long breath. "I said something like 'You got your nerve, prowling around in the dark and scarin' the wits half out of a man. What the hell do you want?' "

Kirby shook his head slowly. "Come now, Sheriff. Those weren't your exact words, now, were they?"

"Near enough."

"Remember that you're under oath. Tell us exactly what you said."

Murtry's body slumped and his eyes cast downward. "I said, 'What the hell do you want, *Rule?*' "

A loud murmur swept through the crowd. Kirby swung around and pointed a finger at Rule. "It was this man who drew you outside, wasn't it, Sheriff?"

"I thought it was him," Murtry said, "but now I ain't so sure. Hard to tell. I wouldn't stake a man's life on it. Anyway, it's all fuzzy in my recollection, because I only saw him for a second. Before I could get a good look, someone come up behind me and gave me this lump." Murtry gingerly dabbed at the swelling on the back of his head. "After that, I didn't see nothing till I came to some time later."

Kirby nodded and made a low, sympathetic sound. "And that is when you discovered that a tragedy had occurred?"

Murtry nodded.

"I found McAllister was dead."

"How did he die, Sheriff?"

Murtry stole a glance in Rule's direction, then he faced front again and sighed. "He was hanged. The rope was tossed over a rafter and he was swinging from it, dead as a stone."

Kirby paced by the table where Taggart sat, reached under it, and held up a coil of rope for everyone to see. "Hanged with this very rope." He took it forward and showed it to Murtry. "I ask you to identify it for us, Sheriff. You will note it is of unusual quality and workmanship."

Murtry barely glanced down. "Yeah, that's the one."

Kirby dropped the rope on the judge's desk. "Your Honor, I ask that this be placed in evidence. Now, Sheriff, you know to whom this particular rope belongs, don't you? Didn't you, in fact, know of its existence even before it was used to brutally murder Tom McAllister?"

"I'd heard of it," Murtry said.

Winslow spoke up quickly. "Objection."

"I'll rephrase the question," Kirby said smoothly. "Sheriff, would you kindly tell us who told you about this rope?"

"Rule did."

A loud buzzing shot through the crowd. Kirby raised his hand to silence them before the judge could react. Then he turned back to Murtry. "Tell us, Sheriff, the circumstances in which you heard about the rope now in evidence."

Murtry nodded glumly. "It was when we arrested McAllister. Rule told him, 'I got a special new rope back in my room, just waiting for you.' He was, you know, threatening him with it."

"Your Honor?" Winslow pleaded. "Now the witness is offering conclusions."

The judge shook his head. "I'll allow it. Please continue, Sheriff."

"Where was I?" Murtry asked. "I think I was done."

Kirby stepped up in front of his witness. "Not quite, Sheriff. That was not the only occasion on which Rule threatened and harassed your prisoner, was it?"

"No, I guess there was one other time."

"Indeed there was. One other time when Rule was so harsh and abusive to McAllister—a prisoner of the law, trapped in a jail cell and unable to escape or defend himself from those threats—that you, in fact, felt obligated to ban Rule from ever visiting the prisoner again. Isn't that so?"

"Yeah, that's right. I did do that."

"Why? What did Rule say to make you banish him from the jail?"

"I can tell you exactly what he said. Rule told him, 'I'm gonna hang you, McAllister. And no judge or court in the world can stop me.' "

"He actually said that? 'No *judge or court*'? You're quite sure he used those words?" Kirby shook his head as if appalled beyond belief.

"That's right. He said, 'Nothing can save you from me. Next time we face each other, I'll be slipping a noose around your neck.' "

"Is that all, Sheriff?"

"Well . . ." Murtry said hesitantly.

Kirby pressed him, "Didn't he in fact say one thing more?"

Murtry glanced at Rule with a sorrowful look, then wheezed in a long deep breath. "That's right—he said, 'And I'm gonna enjoy it.' "

The onlookers buzzed like angry hornets. Kirby turned and smiled at Winslow. "Your witness, sir."

For a moment it appeared that Winslow hadn't heard him. He didn't get to his feet or even look up. Murtry squirmed a little on his chair, and the judge's face creased in a hard frown. Then, just as the judge opened his mouth to speak, Winslow raised his head. His voice had little of Kirby's boom and thunder, but what it lacked in volume, it made up for with bite.

"Where did you eat supper on the night before McAllister was killed?"

Murtry looked up sharply. "What's that got to do with anything?"

"Didn't you, in fact, spend a considerable portion of the evening in the saloon?"

"I always eat my supper at the saloon. That's no secret. But I didn't get drunk, if that's what you're tryin' to say. I was eating."

"Then I am impressed by your appetite, Sheriff. Since you were in the saloon from six o'clock until nearly eleven. That's true, isn't it?"

"Maybe I was. I deserve some time off, same as any workin' man. And if I want to relax in that time with a few drinks, it's no one's business but mine."

"So you did have a few drinks, maybe even several?"

"Yeah, so what if I did?" Murtry grumbled.

Winslow said, "And then you went back to work. Tell me, Sheriff, what would you think of a working man who drinks *before* reporting to his job?"

Deighton Kirby sprang from his chair. "Objection!"

"I withdraw the question," Winslow said, smiling slightly. "You've been very patient, Sheriff. There is just one final matter I would like to clear up, if we may."

"Thank God," Murtry sighed.

"Sheriff, you said that the man who knocked on your door retreated to the shadows where he was hard to make out. That's not the way Mr. Rule normally presented himself, was it?"

Murtry shook his head. "No, course not."

"Can you imagine any reason why a man in those circumstances would act so oddly? Why he would take such pains to keep you from seeing his face?"

Kirby shot up again. "Your Honor, please?"

"I'll rephrase my question," Winslow said quickly. "Sheriff, didn't you wonder why the man was hiding his face?"

"No, sir," Murtry admitted. He looked over at Rule and lowered his voice almost to a whisper. "I never did."

*   *   *

The lawyers fascinated Randy. To him they seemed like two angry boys trying to outargue each other, one saying the nastiest thing he could think of, then the other shooting back with something even worse. Winslow was plenty game and gave near as good as he got, but the odds were stacked against him. Kirby put one witness after another on the stand, and there was hardly anything Winslow could say to them.

Johnson came next. He was the young man staying at Mrs. Hardt's boardinghouse who was always looking for a job but somehow never finding one.

"Tell us, Mr. Johnson," Kirby said, "what you heard when you were awakened early last Saturday morning."

"I heard Rule thumpin' around in his room. That's what woke me up in the first place. He banged around for a spell, then I heard him stomp down the stairs. I thought it was downright unneighborly of him to be so unconcerned about disturbing the sleep of others."

"And what time did all this occur, would you say?"

"It was a quarter after three," Johnson replied. "I know, 'cause I looked at my watch."

"You're quite certain you heard Rule leave at that time? You couldn't be mistaken?"

"If'n somebody woke you at such an ungodly hour, you'd remember it, wouldn't you?"

Kirby smiled. "Yes, I believe I would. Thank you, Mr. Johnson.

Winslow took a crack at him then. "This commotion you heard from Rule's room—how can you be certain he was the one making it? Couldn't the same noises have been made by someone else, say someone searching through Rule's things, looking for something? A rope, perhaps."

Johnson pursed his lips and chewed on that thought for a minute, then said, "I suppose it could have been. But it weren't."

"You admitted you didn't see anyone—how can you be so certain he was the one creating the noise?"

"It came from his room. Who else could it have been?"

Winslow smiled. "Yes, that is an interesting question."

After that, things just got worse. The witnesses came fast, one right after the other.

"Your personal opinion of the defendant's character is not the issue, Mrs. Hardt. Please answer the question."

"No sir, Mr. Rule never complained to me about anything stolen from his room."

"Your witness, Mr. Winslow."

"No questions."

"You say the defendant violently attacked you, Mr. Taggart?"

"He held a knife to my throat in front of the whole town. You can see the mark right here."

"And you personally heard Mr. Rule threaten the life of Tom McAllister on more than one occasion?"

"Only every time I saw him."

"Mr. Winslow?"

"No questions, Your Honor."

"Mr. Greene, are you quite certain you did nothing to provoke the defendant into assaulting you?"

"No sir, not a thing."

"Didn't you attempt to reason with him?"

"He nearly throttled me. Damned hard to talk with thumbs in your throat, mister."

"Thank you, sir."

The judge's eyes widened when he saw the defense attorney climb to his feet. "Ah, Mr. Winslow, do I take it you thought of a question?"

"Just one. Mr. Greene, do you know what the word *perjury* means?"

"Ain't that something to do with ladies' undies?"

"Never mind."

"Well, you asked."

Soon after that, Kirby announced that the prosecution rested. The judge seemed very pleased by this news. "The court wishes to extend its gratitude to you, Mr. Kirby, for a well-considered and admirably succinct presentation. Your turn, Mr. Winslow. Call your first witness, please."

Winslow got to his feet slowly, and it was clear from the grim look on his face that things weren't going his way. "I wish to beg the court's indulgence," he said. "The defense is unable to present any witnesses at this time."

The judge frowned. "Did I hear you correctly, sir?"

"I respectfully request a one-day recess, so that I may locate and persuade certain reluctant persons to step forward."

"Young man, this is unconscionable," the judge snapped. "Do you mean to tell me you have prepared no case at all?"

"Your Honor, all of my potential witnesses have either disappeared or have refused to appear out of fear for their own personal safety."

"Then what difference would another day make, Mr. Winslow? Frankly, I am appalled by the effrontery of such a request. Make your case now or not at all."

"Your Honor, my hands are tied. My witnesses are afraid to appear. And I am reluctant to coerce them, because the threat against them is real and considerable."

"That is enough," the judge said. "You can't make up for inadequate preparation by bandying accusations and innuendo, young man. I demand that you produce a witness."

Winslow sighed. "Your Honor, I am unable to do that."

"You have the defendant. Put him on the stand. Surely the man can speak for himself."

"Respectfully, sir, it is my opinion that such an appearance would not be in my client's best interests."

The judge scowled and shook his head. "Your opinion is a

matter of singular unimportance to me at the moment, young man. As to your client's best interests—I can only extend to him my sympathy for not having procured better legal counsel. I will not allow you to waste any more time. Either put him on the stand, or I will render a decision on the basis of the testimony heard thus far."

"Your Honor, I must protest your interference with the presentation of my case."

"Mr. Winslow, you haven't offered a case to interfere with. This is your last chance. Now, what's it going to be?"

Winslow seemed to fold up inside his suit. He hung his head and sighed. "You leave me no choice. The defense calls Ulysses Rule."

CHAPTER 21

RANDY'S heart sank as he watched Rule make his way to the witness chair. It wasn't fair, somehow everything had gone wrong; the judge would never take Rule's word over all those other witnesses. Randy glanced around, praying that somebody, anybody, would stand up and offer to tell the truth on Rule's behalf. Someone had to speak for him, they just had to—otherwise, it was all over.

But he knew it wasn't going to happen. There was no one who could help Rule. No one but him.

Just then Sarah tugged gently on Randy's arm, and motioned with her head toward the back. He looked that way and saw his father amidst the crowd in the doorway, waving for them to join him.

Randy grabbed his mother's hand as she started to stand. "We can't go now. Don't you see what's goin' on up there?"

"Remember your promise," she said in a stern whisper. "No backtalk, come on now."

Randy reluctantly stood up and started to follow her. Bill Kitson looked over and grinned. "What's the matter, can't ya take it no more? You really are a sissy-boy, ain't ya?"

"You and me are through, Bill," Randy said. "I can find a better friend than you."

Bill pondered his reply for a moment, and finally just stuck out his tongue.

"Will you come on?" Sarah's tug this time wasn't gentle. People stared as she half dragged him down the row of chairs. Two men growled at Randy when he stepped on their boots.

"About time," Callum said when they finally made their

way to his side. "I thought I'd have to stand there forever before one of you would look my way."

He moved them outside quickly, his strong arms clearing a way through the people all milling around for a better look inside. The wagon was parked nearby. Callum said, "Climb up, boy. It's time for us to move on."

Randy didn't move. "Pa, we can't go yet. You didn't see what went on in there."

"I saw enough. That Winslow fella's made a real mess of things. But don't you worry, son. It'll be all right. Rule has a chance to speak his piece now."

Randy shook his head. "No, he can't do that. Rule can't go on that stand. It's the worst thing that could happen."

"Why's that?"

"If he does, the other lawyer gets to ask him questions, too. All Kirby has to do is ask him: 'Is this your rope?' Rule will have to say yes. And it'll all be over."

"You caught on to that lawyer business quick, didn't you?" Callum said, sounding half-pleased despite himself.

"Rule's in a bad spot, Pa. Someone has to speak up for him or he's a goner."

"Nothing we can do about that. I'm sorry about this whole business, but Rule brought it upon himself. Now, get on the wagon like I told you."

"Pa, please . . . we can't just leave him."

"You heard me. Get a move on."

Sarah said softly, "Dan? Are you sure we're doing the right thing?"

Callum raised his head and frowned at her. "Not you, too. Don't I have enough to worry about?"

"I don't feel good about running away."

"Sarah, we're doing the *only* thing we can. You know that." He turned and took Randy by the arm. "Now get on that wagon, or so help me, I'll throw you on it."

Randy wrenched his arm free and shouted, "No! It's not right, it's not right at all!"

Callum reached out for the boy again, but Randy twisted free. Before his father could stop him, he dashed back toward the Union Hall.

"Stay here," Callum ordered Sarah. "I'll bring him back before he kills us all."

He was right on Randy's heels when he reached the doorway, but from there the boy had an edge. The door was blocked by a logjam of people. Callum had to nudge and shove people out of his way, while Randy just ducked down and squirmed straight through.

Randy burst into the courtroom and ran down the center aisle. In a glance, he saw Rule on the witness chair, Winslow close by. Both men were staring at him. Rule was pale and seemed upset by Randy's appearance. The boy stopped short, suddenly aware that he was the focus of attention. He heard the room go quiet and people on both sides turned to stare at him.

The judge pounded his gavel, even though no one was making a sound. "Young man, what is the meaning of this interruption?"

He sounded angry, and his hostile gaze made Randy feel small and unsure of himself. His mouth went dry with sudden fear.

"Well? Speak up, boy."

Taggart shot to his feet. "Get that brat out of here!" he snarled.

Randy felt a hand on his shoulder, and spun around anxiously. With relief, he saw it was his father. "Come with me, son. Please, boy. You don't know what you're doing." Then he looked up at the judge. "I apologize, Your Honor. I'll just take him out now and—"

"No! I'm not goin'."

Randy brushed his father's hand away. With sudden determination, he turned back and faced the judge. "My name is Randy Callum, and I got something to say. The truth needs to be told here, and you can pound that hammer till you're blue in the face, but I'm not leavin' till it's said."

"Well, you certainly are a spirited young man." The judge smiled faintly and looked at Kirby and Winslow. "Counselors, can either of you help me out with this?"

Winslow stepped forward. "Your Honor, I ask that you allow him to be heard." Rule hissed at him, but he went on anyway. "This brave youth has stepped forward at no small risk to himself. It would be a mockery of justice if you did not hear him out."

"This is *your* witness, Mr. Winslow?" the judge asked.

"Your Honor, I protest," Kirby said. "I've not yet had an opportunity to cross-examine the current witness."

"I've granted you considerable latitude, sir. It is only fair the defense be given equal consideration." The judge frowned and scratched his beard in a thoughtful manner. "Mr. Winslow, do you wish to change horses at this point and put the young man on the stand?"

"I do, Your Honor."

"Very well. Young man, step forward."

Randy walked slowly down the aisle to the front of the courtroom. Rule shook his head at him as they passed each other. Randy pretended he didn't notice.

Vickers turned the boy to face the crowd, then put a Bible under his left hand. Randy raised his right hand and swore to tell the whole truth. Then he sat down on the witness chair. Glancing around as he settled himself, Randy saw his father, still standing in the middle of the aisle. He looked as if he were going to be sick.

Winslow approached Randy and said in a gentle voice, "Now, son, don't be nervous. Just tell us the truth in your own words. Ready?"

Randy nodded.

"All right, here goes. You know beyond any doubt that Mr. Rule, the defendant here, did not commit the murder of Tom McAllister. Isn't that a fact?"

"Yessir, it is."

Winslow smiled. "Please tell us how it is you know that."

Randy gulped and swallowed hard. "Well, sir, the time they say the murder happened, Rule couldn't have done it."

"Why not, Randall?"

" 'Cause . . . at that time, he was with me."

A buzz of loud whispering sounded from the crowd. The judge slammed down his gavel.

"Fine, Randall," Winslow said. "You're doing very well. Where were you and Mr. Rule in the hours before sunrise on Saturday last?"

"We were on our way to the mine," Randy answered. "I led Mr. Rule up there, to make sure he didn't get lost. We left a couple hours before sunup, so as to get a good start."

"Did Mr. Rule tell you why he wanted to go to the mine?"

"Yes, he wanted to find out about the business McAllister was involved in. He said he suspected that McAllister and Mr. Taggart were up to something dishonest."

"Objection!" Kirby shouted. "Your Honor, Mr. Taggart is not on trial here."

"Overruled," the judge said. To Winslow, he added, "I will allow it, but I advise you to tread carefully, sir. You had better be certain where you're going with this."

"I am quite certain, Your Honor," Winslow said. He turned back to Randy quickly. "Tell us, did Mr. Rule learn anything to prove his suspicions were correct?"

"Yeah, he sure did." Randy raised his head and looked back at all the people watching him. "He learned that McAllister was writin' false assay reports, claimin' that the ore is a lot higher grade than it really is."

Taggart slammed his fist down on the table. "That is preposterous!"

The crowd hummed with confused mutters of disbelief.

The judge pounded his gavel several times before the noise died down. He looked at Kirby and said, "Advise your associate to restrain himself, sir. I will tolerate no more outbursts."

"The boy's testimony is irrelevant," Kirby said smoothly. "I ask that it be stricken from the record."

Winslow faced the judge and said, "I am attempting to establish motive, sir. I intend to prove that Tom McAllister was involved in a scheme of fraud which Rule threatened to uncover, and that the murder was an attempt to prevent that scheme from being disclosed."

The judge's eyes opened wide. He stared at Winslow for a minute, then said, "I'll permit the testimony to stand. Please continue."

"Thank you, Your Honor." Winslow turned back to the boy. "This is very important, Randall. Take your time and tell us exactly what you remember. What did Rule learn was the purpose of those falsified assay reports?"

"They was meant to make the mine appear more productive and profitable." Randy paused, glanced at Taggart, then looked away quickly and took a deep breath. "So he and Mr. Taggart could sell it out."

"That's a lie!" Taggart yelled. He was on his feet, shaking his fist. "Get that boy out of here. I won't stand here and listen to his filthy lies."

That brought the house down. Suddenly, everybody was talking all at once.

"Order, I will have order," the judge yelled. He pounded his gavel but hardly anyone could hear him. "Mr. Kirby, make that man sit down. One more disturbance from him and I will have him forcibly removed."

Taggart didn't budge. "He's the one you ought to toss out," he cried, pointing a finger at Randy. "The brat's just making it all up. He can't prove a thing."

"Can so," Randy shouted back. "You're selling to an Eastern syndicate, and their front man is a fella named Coleson. Ask him if you don't believe me."

Winslow spun around and called, "Is there a Mr. Coleson here?"

A figure at the back got slowly to his feet. Everybody turned to stare at him. "Yes, my name is Coleson," he said. "What the boy said is—"

Then suddenly everybody was screaming. Taggart leapt up to the front, Greene and Younger right behind him. They all had guns in their hands and waved them at the crowd.

"Sit still, all of you," Taggart yelled. "I'll kill the first man that twitches." He pulled Randy up by his hair, and touched the gun to his head. "We're getting out of here now. Nobody gets in our way, nobody follows."

Randy squirmed, but Taggart just pressed the gun harder against his head and half picked him off the floor. Greene and Younger kept the crowd still while Taggart backed toward the side door, shielding himself with Randy's body.

Then they were outside in the alley. Taggart took a grip on the boy's shirt and made him stumble along with him as they ran for the street. His two henchmen pounded up right behind. A fearful commotion sounded in the background as people fled from the courtroom, screaming and fighting among themselves.

Taggart stopped at the end of the alley to glance down the street. Dozens of horses were hitched outside the Union Hall. Randy gulped, realizing Taggart and his men could take their pick and be gone before anyone could stop them.

Then he spotted his mother, still waiting beside the wagon. With a terrified look on her face, she was watching all the people stream from the Union Hall. Something caught her eye and she glanced their way, saw Randy with Taggart's gun at his head, and her body convulsed as though she had been struck in the stomach.

Taggart gave Randy's hair a vicious yank. "Come on, damn you! Stop dragging your feet."

"Ma!" Randy yelled. But Taggart was pulling him away, and he couldn't see her reaction.

The three outlaws fanned out and headed into the street. But just then Sarah whipped the horses into motion, driving the team and wagon straight at them. Taggart swore and dove back in the alley as tons of horseflesh bore down on him.

At the last second the horses spooked and reared up, kicking as if they were fighting off a pack of wolves. A flying hoof struck Younger across the face and he went down hard.

Randy saw his chance. While Taggart was ducking from the horses, he lowered his face to the hand clutching his shirt and sank his teeth in soft flesh.

Taggart screamed and pistol-whipped him across the side of the head. Randy lay sprawled on the ground. Taggart loomed over him, sucking on his chewed hand, and took careful aim. "You little son of a bitch. You asked for this!"

Then in sudden amazement, Randy saw Taggart being lifted right up in the air. He dangled there a moment, clean off his feet, and it was then Randy saw his father behind him. Taggart went soaring backward through the air, arms and legs thrashing wildly.

He smashed into the outside of the Union Hall, hard enough to splinter the planks, and sort of hung there, limp and dazed. His gun dropped harmless in the dust.

Callum closed on him and buried a fist in Taggart's stomach. The big man's breath wheezed out and he started to double over, but Callum straightened him up again with a blow to the face. Then another, and another. Taggart's head flopped from side to side, and the only thing that kept him standing was the force of those terrible hammerlike punches.

Randy's father was like a crazy man as he mercilessly pounded Taggart again and again. The muscles in Callum's arms stood out like chiseled stone as his fist thudded into the big meaty body. Taggart's face was a bloody mess.

The sight scared Randy. He dove on his father's back and pulled him away. "No, Pa. That's enough. You'll *kill* him!"

Callum spun around with his fist still poised, and for a

minute Randy thought he would take a swing at him. Then all at once the wildness faded from his eyes. He stared at his own fist as if it were something that belonged to somebody else.

"You all right, son?" he asked in a breathless whisper.

Randy didn't say anything, just threw his arms around his father and hugged him as if he'd never let go ever again. Then Callum said what Randy thought sounded like the sweetest words in all the world. "Come on, son. Let's go home."

They turned away, arm in arm. But they had taken only one step when a small but ugly sound stopped them. The dry click of a gun hammer.

They turned around and saw Taggart behind them. His face was covered in blood and he was weaving badly, but the gun in his hand looked steady enough to take seriously. "Couldn't keep your noses out of my business," Taggart spat. "But now you're going to pay for it."

Suddenly, for no apparent reason, he just toppled over like a felled tree. Randy looked up and saw Murtry standing over him. The sheriff grinned and hefted the heavy old Sharps he'd clubbed Taggart with. "Damn, got it wrong again, didn't I?" he said. "I never can remember which end of this thing you're supposed to use."

And, just like that, it was all over.

CHAPTER 22

SARAH came running, gathered Randy into her arms, and hugged and kissed him. He was too relieved at being rescued and safe even to feel embarrassed. Then Callum gently pried them apart and asked Sarah if she would drive the wagon home. "Randy and I will be along directly to unload it," he said.

Sarah was so pleased by those few words that they had to repeat all the hugs and kisses one more time. But finally she got on the wagon and rode off, waving happily.

Callum put his arm proudly around Randy's shoulders. It wasn't until then that the boy looked up and realized there were people standing all around, grinning at them. His face flushed red from all the attention.

Rule and Winslow were among the crowd, and their smiles were the warmest of all. Callum and Randy walked over to them. For a long time they all stood grinning at one another and couldn't think of anything to say. Then Callum went up to Rule and stuck out his hand. "We nearly made a terrible mistake. I hope you can find it in your heart to forgive us."

"Nonsense," Rule said. "I'm the one who should be thanking you." When he shook Callum's hand the crowd laughed, because they saw Rule's wrists were still cuffed together.

Murtry and his deputies came out from the alley, marching his three prisoners to the jail. Taggart was weaving like a drunk, and neither Greene nor Younger looked in much better shape. Murtry called his group to a halt and strolled over. He dug a key from his pocket and slipped the cuffs off Rule's hands.

"Hope you don't mind. I think I found a better use for these."

Rule rubbed his chafed wrists and said, "I'd call it square if you let me watch the door swing shut on that lot. I like to see things to the end."

"Yeah, I know you do," Murtry said. "Sure, come along." He turned to Randy and his father. "Why don't you-all join us? Without you, the parade won't seem complete."

"Pa?" Randy said.

Callum patted him on the back and nodded. "Go ahead, son. I'll see you later at home."

So they all marched off together. Murtry had been joking, but the truth was it did seem like a parade. Nearly the whole town was lined up on the boardwalks, and when they passed by, the people started to clap. Randy had never known a simple noise could be so beautiful and stirring. He swelled up with pride until he feared he would burst.

The usual faces were outside the saloon. When Randy drew near, Gus Barker stepped from the crowd and yelled out to him, "Hey, boy! Catch."

He tossed something through the air. Randy snagged it, then held it up. A shiny new dime gleamed in his hand.

Barker laughed and said, "Keep it, boy. This is the second time I learned it was wrong to bet against you. It's not gonna happen again."

Randy waved at him gratefully, and the parade continued a short distance more, then drew to a halt outside the feed store. Randy was almost sorry to see it all end. Murtry led the prisoners inside, then Rule and the boy followed.

After all the noise and attention, the small room seemed unnaturally quiet. "You boys grab a chair," Murtry told his deputies. "I'll see to this, personal." He gave Taggart a shove in the back to steer him toward the cells.

Rule and Randy tagged behind him. They didn't go all the way into the corridor, but hung back a respectful distance. They could still see Taggart and the other two when the doors slammed shut on them, and that was all they had come for. Murtry turned back to his audience and smiled. "That felt good," he said. "You know, I might actually learn to enjoy this job yet."

"It does have its rewards," Rule told him. "Well, Sheriff, you need any help holding them? Or am I free to go?"

Murtry strolled down their way. "Aren't you going to stay for the new trial?" he asked. "We might wind up in need of a hangman, you know."

Rule shook his head. "No, thanks. Not really my concern. And I've seen as much of a courtroom as I care to."

"Guess I can understand that," Murtry said. He half stumbled, as his boot knocked into the lantern, which had been carelessly left on the floor. He bent over and picked it up. "I swear I don't know why folks don't put things back where they found 'em," he muttered, and stuck the lantern back up on its wall hook.

Something about those words jarred Randy. He looked at Rule and said, "Why, that's just where you left it that day you told McAllister you were going to hang him and enjoy it—"

Then he saw the look on Rule's face and his voice died in his throat.

Murtry shuffled by into the office. "I'm gonna pour myself some coffee. You comin'?"

"In a minute," Rule said.

"Suit yourself. Just lock the door tight when you come."

He disappeared through the doorway and they were alone.

Randy looked up at Rule and it took every ounce of his courage to form the words. "*You* didn't do it, did you?"

Rule sighed, then reached out and put his hand on the boy's shoulder. "I *could* have. You know that, don't you?" he said.

Randy stared at him. After a second, he reached up and threw off his hand.

Rule nodded and turned away. At the doorway he stopped but didn't turn around. His voice was hardly more than a whisper. "You did a good thing today, Mr. Callum," he said. "Be proud."

"I thought so once," Randy said, and glared at him. "Now I'm not so sure."

Rule let his breath out in a long sigh, then turned away. And was gone. Randy never saw him again.

It was nearly a week later when the real story finally came out. The morning of Taggart's trial the townspeople awoke to find Murtry was nowhere to be found. Younger came clean and explained what happened. He said that Taggart got desperate and offered the sheriff a bribe to let him escape— and Murtry accepted. He took Taggart's money and just ran off with it, leaving Taggart a little less wealthy and still in jail. Murtry had joked with Rule that if someone would offer him a bribe he'd be gone so fast it would make your head spin. It turned out he was a man of his word.

The bribery attempt was what persuaded Younger to start talking. Taggart had bargained for his own escape only, and would have left Younger and Greene behind without a second thought. Younger saw that. Even a stone will crack if you beat on it often enough. Younger turned evidence against the other two and spilled the whole story. He said the killing had been Taggart's doing. Younger claimed all he did was lure Murtry outside, then hide his face in the shadows until Greene sneaked up and knocked the sheriff cold. He'd worn a cloak like Rule's and smoked tobacco they'd stolen from Rule's room along with the rope they used to hang McAllister.

Taggart had been mightily pleased with the cleverness of his plan, Younger said, framing the meddlesome Rule and getting rid of an unwanted partner—thus keeping McAllister's share of syndicate money for himself—all in one night's work. The murder, after all, had been about nothing but money. Younger said Taggart had called it "just good business."

Randy felt sick with regret. His suspicion about Rule had been misguided. Despite all his hate and lust for revenge, Rule had done nothing wrong.

This revelation wasn't much comfort. Randy felt cheated. Rule was a man he had looked up to and had come to regard as a friend. But the manner of Rule's departure convinced him he'd been wrong about that. Real friends don't cast each other aside so lightly.

"I just don't understand it," Randy muttered. "I thought he cared what I thought about him. I looked up to him."

Sarah said, "A man who hunts down other men and hangs them is no one to admire." Then a thoughtful look came across her face, and her voice softened. "You know, I think that's what Rule tried to tell you. It's not easy to live up to someone else's opinion. Maybe he didn't want to be anyone's hero."

Randy's father left without a word and walked out the door. A few minutes later, he came back with the rope that had been used to hang McAllister. Sarah frowned but he stilled her protest with a sharp look. Randy stared at the coil and shook his head. "I don't want that."

"Keep it anyway. Not to remind you of Rule, but of what he stood for. He called it justice. To my mind it's something else. But you decide."

Randy took one end of the rope.

"Stretch it," Callum ordered.

Randy grabbed with both hands and tugged and strained. "There's no play in it," he grunted. "It won't give an inch."

Callum smiled faintly. "It takes more pull than you or I could muster, but it will give. A rope's no good without play. You know what that is, son? Tolerance."

Randy looked up at his father. "I think I do."

"Rule made a decision a long time ago to let nothing stand in the way of revenge, not even friendship. He can't give an inch without feeling he's backed down. It's a poor trade-off, and makes him a hard man. Maybe he has to be that way to do what he does. But it's not the way for all men. When you think of Rule, remember his strength and his courage, but measure them against the tolerance he lacks." Callum gently pushed the coil into his son's hands. "That's all I ask."

Every day since the mine had been shut down one or two more families had packed up and moved on. Bannon had always been a quiet town, but now it was on its way to a mournful silence. The trial of Taggart and Greene didn't draw the crowd that Rule's had. The Union Hall was barely more than half full. But what the spectators lacked in number, they made up with bitterness. The federal marshals had to rush Taggart and Greene out under armed guard.

Ten days later Taggart and Greene were hanged side by side on the gallows that Rule had paid to build. Folks said it was the most gruesome and memorable sight they'd ever witnessed, something they'd never, ever forget. But of course Randy only had their word on that.

He stayed home.

If you have enjoyed this book and would like to receive details about other Walker Western titles, please write to:

Western Editor
Walker and Company
720 Fifth Avenue
New York, NY 10019